Earthquakes & Butterflies

First published in 2015
Reprinted 2016

Copyright © Kathleen Gallagher 2015
The moral right of the author has been asserted

A catalogue record for this book is available from
the National Library of New Zealand.

ISBN 978-0-473-33232-7

A catalogue record for this book is available from the
National Library of New Zealand

All rights reserved. No part of this book may be reproduced or
transmitted in any form or by any means, electronic or mechanical,
including photocopying, recording or by any information storage and
retrieval system without prior permission in writing from the publisher.

Proudly printed in New Zealand by Printlink

Published by Wickcandle
33 Crichton Tce
Cashmere
Christchurch
New Zealand

www.wickcandle.co.nz

For discussion group facebook Earthquakes and Butterflies

EARTHQUAKES & BUTTERFLIES

Otautahi Christchurch

4 September 2010 Magnitude 7.1
13611 aftershocks

22 February 2011 Magnitude 6.4
9183 aftershocks

13 June 2011 Magnitude 6.3
5241 aftershocks

23 December 2011 Magnitude 6.2
3317 aftershocks

BY KATHLEEN GALLAGHER

PHOTOGRAPHS MICHAEL COUGHLAN

DESIGN KATY YIAKMIS

Me rere koutou he pūrerehua ki ngā rangi
Me huaki a tātou kanohi ki ngā māramatanga o ngā whetu

Fly like a butterfly through the heavens
Open our eyes to the wisdom of the stars

For Joanna Clare Didham, Jamie Gilbert, Eileen Coughlan, Kieran Gallagher-Power, Murray Parsons, Allan Boote, Noel Wakefield, Mollie McGrade Clark, Mary Gallagher, Lorraine Doyle, Helen Stribling, Elizabeth O'Connor and all of our loved ones who died or were injured in accidents, became seriously ill, or died prematurely, in, during, and following the epicentre shifting sequence of 30,000 earthquakes, including 25 major earthquakes (shallower than 10 metres and greater than 5.2 magnitude), that shook Otautahi Christchurch to its very bones beginning on 4 September 2010.

High Street

1

~Rūaumoko~

Earthquake atua
Youngest child
of Papatuanuku
& Ranginui

Everything talks with me nowadays. Nothing is separate. There is no distance between us. No thick veil blocks the natural world from the human world. All of the air is fresh and thin. A bumblebee comes into the room, ambles around, having a chat. A fly crawls up my arm, a seagull sits down beside me, not even standing on its legs, just sits, all fluffed up, gazing into my eyes.

When the tectonic plate splits, blue and white lights appear, two, three, four hours before it is about to happen. The tectonic plate splits in only five per cent of the world's earthquakes. This is a natural part of the earth's growing process, her expansion, her stretching and her breaking open.

Time is no longer linear. Time contracts and expands. Inside the time frame of an earthquake shaking for one minute can feel like one hour. Some things are seen before they happen and other things appear after they have happened, clear as day. Terror replaces any subtle feelings. Doing over-rides sequential thinking. Each action is separate, discrete. I write this journal to re-member myself.

A tall young man with a mop of black wavy hair crouches in the middle of the street, away from the shop facades crashing around him. He watches from under his hands. People are screaming, crying, calling out, coughing, running, standing still, some motionless. The ground is scattered with broken bricks, rock, glass, clothes and shoes.

He looks carefully through the rising dust and sees another young man high up on the scaffolding. The scaffolding is waving in and out from the building with each huge shake. The young man on the scaffolding wears a hard hat. Loses his balance, reaches out, grabs a scaffolding pole and slips down the pole. His leg catches on a rung. He loses his grip. He falls and is held only by his leg. When the next big quake comes he is knocked out against the pole. Loses consciousness. He is left dangling in the air.

Hone sits quietly waiting in the middle of High Street. When the next quake comes, he stays there until the shaking subsides. Then he picks his way across the rocks and bits of broken shop front to the bottom of the broken scaffolding. He makes his way up the scaffolding to the place where the young man is hanging by his foot.

Hone perches on the rung above the young man, he reaches down and takes hold of his arm and pulls him up onto his shoulders. Hone makes his way carefully down the scaffolding with the unconscious young man on his back. When they are almost at the bottom, Hone's right foot catches under a piece of wood sticking out of the scaffolding. He tries to pull his foot out from under the piece of wood. It won't budge. He twists his foot and pulls it out of his shoe.

Hone doesn't see where his shoe goes, but the shoe spins up and into the air, out onto the middle of the street. His right foot is shoeless. Another shake comes. The two young men are thrown about. The scaffolding holds. Hone has the young man securely on his shoulders. With one shoe on, Hone makes his way down to the ground. Then a huge aftershock comes and a brick wall collapses on top of both of them.

Our Lady in Catholic Cathedral turret window

2

~Te Whaea~

Mother Mary

Before the earthquakes there was some distance, some distinction between myself and the sky, but now the clouds, the brilliant red sunsets, the soft cloudy evenings, weave their way inside of me. I am struck by their soft white grey, their brilliant red orange intensity. I am consumed. As if clouds, wind, stars and moon have all awakened inside me and there's no going back. Our earth, Papatuanuku, is a living, breathing ocean. Everything about her is fluid. For some brief periods of time she gives the appearance of solidity.

The acceleration in the February 2011 earthquake occurs mainly in a vertical direction with many people being tossed into the air. Seismic waves rebounding off the hard basalt of the Cashmere Hills back into the city, contribute to the immense ground acceleration.

Kara is on her way into the city. She has just crossed Moorhouse Ave and is on Barbadoes Street when the quake catches her. Her breath stops, she feels an echoing hollowness deep inside her. The lampposts are waving oddly, the stoplights are bouncing around as if they were made of rubber, the cars are zigzagging drunkenly. Traffic comes to a grinding halt. The tar sealed roads crack. Cars tip into the deep cracks. People clamber out onto the road.

As the shaking continues on, becoming wilder and wilder, Kara feels her stomach turn inside out. Her whole spine tingles up and down. She wonders where her two sons Hone and Hemi are at this very moment. She prays. She looks up at the Cathedral of the Blessed Sacrament and watches as the right turret cracks and partly falls. She moves back to the other side of the road. The magnificent copper domes expand and inflate as if they are breathing in and out. The tall white stone pillars sway backwards and forwards like the limbs of a tree in a storm. The turrets of the Cathedral rock, but the left turret does not fall. Kara looses her balance and falls to the ground.

Kara watches in awe as Our Lady appears in the left turret of the Cathedral, before her eyes. As Our Lady appears, the shaking stops. Kara is on the ground, watching Our Lady. Our Lady's hands are outstretched towards the terrified people. Our Lady is facing out over the quaking city, her eyes full of compassion. Near Kara, a small girl asks her Dad, "Who is that?" Her Dad says, "That is Mary, the Mother of Jesus." The small girl waves to Mary. People are running out of their shoes, calling. Shoes are scattered across the streets. Dogs and cats and rats streak away from the shaking buildings. Kara gets to her feet. She helps someone up. She assists someone who is coming, incredibly, out of the Cathedral, to move far away from the openings in the earth and the falling masonry. When they are safe, Kara thanks Our Lady. Kara turns and walks, against the rush of fleeing people into the city. She makes her way to High Street.

She gets there and finds the whole wall fallen through into the place where Hone was working. She searches high and low for signs of life. In the centre of High Street, Kara finds one of Hone's long blue and white running shoes, his right shoe, sitting by itself with no foot in it. She picks it up. It is one of the pair she gave him for his birthday. Kara absentmindedly puts the empty shoe in her bag.

She hears moaning out to the side of the street among bricks and broken masonry. She comes across her son, Hone, lying with another young man still partly on his shoulders. The young man on his shoulders is dead. She checks her son's pulse. She can barely feel it. She takes Hone's head in her lap.

"Hone Hone," she whispers.

She offers water to him. He is unable to swallow. She sits there cradling him. He goes to sleep in her lap. Hone never wakes. Kara prays silently for Hone and the young man on his shoulders. Two deep black fantails piwakawaka fly above Kara and the two young men. Kara can feel the sun on her skin, in her hair, on her tongue. The piwakawaka fly around and around the bricks and broken scaffolding. Then the deep black piwakawaka depart and the soft rain comes, the first decent rain that has fallen in six months. Kara hears the rain falling long and deep, pattering on the ground like it's talking with her.

He purotu koe e taku tama You were conceived my son
No te kahu o te Aoraki As a perfect child of Aoraki
He kahukura koe i te Raki You are now inside the rainbow of the sky
Kokoko i tuha e Bringing the breath of life to all things

Other folk come. They find Kara. They carry the bodies of the two young men out from among the bricks and masonry. They bring Kara out to safety. Kara prays, dear God, keep Hemi, Hone's brother safe somewhere in this quaking city.

Water in foundations, Armagh Street

3

~Wai~
Water
Memory
Song

As the shaking gets bigger, our eyes grow huge and round as saucers. We yell, run, freeze, cry, scream, or stand and grab the nearest post, doorpost, pole, something that we hope and pray won't dance apart.

Some of us stand stock still where we are, freezing in petrified silence, even if it is the wrong place to be. Some folk fall out of bed, or off a chair. Others run outside away from the shaking buildings. At some schools all the children lie down calmly on the waving playing fields outside.

Inside the gap everything shudders wildly, up and down, side to side, heaving, rocking, jumping, roaring, cracking, breaking open. We react on impulse with the roaring of the earth and sky, the shifting lights and everything in between. We enter inside the eternal gap. There is no time inside the gap. Time disappears — it could be twenty seconds, twenty minutes, or twenty hours.

Pieter is on his way home when the first huge earthquake hits. He moves away from the buildings and facades and crouches low. He finds a bike. It's too small. He fumbles with and breaks the lock. The helmet is tiny. He puts the tiny helmet on anyway.

He gets to the bridge over Moorhouse Ave. It is groaning with traffic. He looks up and sees it has been cut off totally from its supporting struts, as if by some huge slicing machine. People in cars are driving over it. Hundreds of others are walking and running under it, as if it is a strong fixed secure surface. It is not as it appears. Miraculously the bridge with the struts totally sheered off, does not collapse on any of the hundreds of people who walk or run under it, nor beneath the hundreds of cars full of people driving over it.

Pieter rides the bike along the road and sometimes on the footpath, zigzagging around the debris and the huge cracks.

There's a big shake while he's riding. He is covered in dust, but he doesn't care. After the next shake he's covered in white dust from head to foot, a tall, white grey ghost on a small bike, knees up, head down inside a white grey helmet.

Pieter winds in and out on the bike. He swerves to miss running people. He reaches the spot, the house, where his wife Kay works doing accounting for an engineering group, two days a week.

He calls out, "Kay, Kay!"

The window is broken. He can hear water pouring from somewhere. Kay is nowhere to be seen. He sees Kay's bright yellow handbag, her good yellow shoes and her skirt and jacket in her office. He picks up her handbag, holds it in his hands.

He wonders if she has gone for a swim. He imagines water slopping in the pool, huge waves, how would she fare on the hard concrete, thrown up like a beached dolphin. Pieter knows she was going somewhere else today, but he can't remember where. There is another shake. A cloud of dust descends. He gets out of the building.

ARTS CENTRE

4

~Piki~

ASCEND

CLIMB OVER, PRESS

CLOSE TOGETHER

HELPER

Because our lifetimes are short we are surprised. We expect the earth to be stable beneath our feet for the seventy or eighty years that we are in our bodies.

If we lived one thousand years, our expectation of the moving and opening and closing of the earth would be different. We would see it as normal for the earth to shudder on occasion, to break open, to pour out molten lava for periods at a time. We would see it as normal for the sea to rise and swallow back in over the land, for the river to change its course and go roaring down a street instead of a riverbed.

Hemi is at work when the first huge earthquake strikes. He is on the thirteenth floor of a building in the Square. The building is rocking sideways and crunching up against the building beside it. Hemi crouches on the floor beside his desk. He reaches under his desk and pulls out his hard climbing hat, throws his rope over his shoulder. He hears wood and metal crunch together. Bits of the staircase collapse.

Hemi unplugs his computer, grabs the hard drive and puts it in his backpack. He goes and sits on the floor in the centre of the building, with his back to the lift well, the strongest part of the building, alongside his workmates. One workmate who was thrown into a cabinet, is holding his ribs.

Hemi waits for the shaking to stop. Then he crawls on all fours over to the window. There is no other way out. Others follow him to the window. He looks down thirteen stories. He ties one end of the rope securely to a post and throws the rest of the rope out the window. He climbs out the window and abseils down the side of the building with his pack on his back.

He lands in the Square — a dark haired young man in a shirt, tie and dishevelled suit, covered in dust with bits of debris in his hair. Others follow him out the window and down the rope. Some have never abseiled in their lives before, and stand frozen by the window. The terrified ones are helped out the window by a woman co-worker, another climber. She gets them down to Hemi on the ground. Hemi waits until everyone is safely down.

Hemi and the woman climber from his office get all the dazed workers from their floor together, and they walk to the Botanical gardens. It is safe there, thank God, beside the trees, away from the buildings.

The cellphone networks are on overload. When everyone is safely settled in the Botanical Gardens, Hemi heads home through the streets towards the hills.

There is a sharp jolt. Hemi moves away from the buildings. He puts the backpack down and picks at the crap on his jacket. He takes the jacket off, shakes it, and puts it on again. There is another shake. Traffic is coming in all directions. He puts the box between his feet and directs the traffic. There is another shake. The traffic stops.

A korimako bellbird flies out of nowhere, swallows tiny insects, which have been disturbed, and hovers in the air above his head. Hemi gazes at the korimako. The korimako gazes back at Hemi.

Cracked wall, Tuam Street

5

~Haruru~

Roar, heavy sound, rumble
Charm to cure wounds

Haruru is the sound that comes. "E haruru ana te ao," The earth is roaring. The haruru comes before, during or after the quaking. The haruru transports you through the realms. This is the realm of earth in which we dwell in our physical bodies. Beneath us is the deeper earth realm and above us, the celestial realm. We, here in this wild quaking middle earth, witness all the comings and goings between the realms.

Ruaumoko was at his mother's breast when Rangi, the sky father of the celestial realm, and she were separated by their older sons, including Tane, the atua of forests. Ruaumoko was given fire for warmth and his movements below cause earthquakes and volcanoes. Earthquakes cause the warmth or cold of Papatuanuku to come to the surface, resulting in the warming or cooling of the earth. Ruaumoko became the husband of Hine-nui-te-po. She is the atua of death. She welcomes the living spirits of her descendants into the world of everlasting light.

Here, in this place, it feels as if all the realms are weaving and heaving together, in and out, around us. The deep and the celestial realms are calling through to us in the middle realms.

Some of us are moving quickly, quietly, unafraid, through the realms.

Pieter is on his bike heading down the road. He sees another man in a dusty suit, standing in the middle of the road directing traffic, a backpack at his feet. Pieter grins from ear to ear. Hemi is alive, thank God. Pieter waves. Hemi waves back and continues directing traffic. Pieter bikes on. He comes to the old people's home. All of the old people are out on the lawn. Some are in their beds, others are in wheelchairs, some are in reclining armchairs.

He finds his mother Helena in a wheelchair. She doesn't know where she is. The nurses and other folk are making cups of tea. Pieter calls to her, as if across a great ocean, "Mama, Mama it was an earthquake. It is all right Mama. You will be all right."

Helena is wringing her hands through her hair.

Earth is bubbling up through the floor. Water is spraying from the ceiling over everything. Pieter looks up. Pipes in the ceilings have burst. Pieter calls to her, "You're going to be all right Mama."

Helena's face is in shock. There is another shake. Helena's face is white, her mouth is open, her eyes full of terror. Her face mirrors how he feels.

Pieter says, "I'll get you to a safe place. This is an earthquake. Remember there have been other earthquakes." Helena's neighbour is Tom. He is 98 years old. Tom lived on the West Coast through the 1929 Murchison earthquake. He also lived through the 1968 Inangahua earthquake. Tom is helping the old people, all of them younger than he is, out of their rooms and into the gardens. He says to Pieter, "We won't truly know what we have lost for eighteen months. " Pieter says, "There is no way we could survive eighteen months of this."

Tom reassures him, "We will survive, Pieter." Helena says nothing. Helena feels to Pieter as if she is some place very far away.

"Have a sip of tea Mama."

Helena can't sip anything. She sits silent and still in her wheelchair, springs of liquefaction coming up from the floor, water pouring down from above her head. There is another quake. Pieter wheels Helena outside through the bubbling liquefaction. He sings to her in their old language, *"Als de lente komt dan stuur ik jou tulpen uit Amsterdam* When spring comes I will send you tulips from Amsterdam *Als de lente kmot pluk ik voor jou tulpen uit Amsterdam* When spring comes I will pick for you tulips from Amsterdam."

Pieter realises Helena is cold. He makes his way back inside through the burst water pipes and the bubbling-up floor. He comes out soaked and with blankets for Helena.

All of the residents from the Rest Home, and the nurses are sitting outside in case the buildings collapse with the next shake. Pieter wraps blankets around Helena. It starts to rain. Some nurses and residents shift back inside. Pieter finds an umbrella and makes a route through the liquefaction and wheels Helena off away down the strangely familiar, unfamiliar street.

Pieter talking more to himself than to Helena, "It's all right Mama. It is all right." But nothing is right. Pieter has no idea what to do, where to take Helena. Helena needs a hoist and full on medical care twenty-four hours a day. Pieter's house is broken through the middle. It doesn't have sewerage or electricity on. He doesn't know if he has enough water for two days. Pieter settles Helena's hair, he sings again, "*Als ik wederkom dan bren ik jou tulpen uit Amsterdam* when I return I will bring you tulips from Amsterdam *Duizend gele, duizend rooie wensen jou het allermooiste* A thousand yellow ones, a thousand red ones, wish you the very best *Wat m'n mond niet zeggen kan zeggen tulpen uit Amsterdam* what my mouth cannot say tulips from Amsterdam will say." Pieter's singing in the old language helps Helena. She becomes more settled.

Pieter walks Helena on down the road, circling the fissures, and the open holes. The pavement is cracked open like a huge dragon-like taniwha has come up out of the river, gnashed its teeth and run its claws through the tar seal, ripped and broken the roads and pavements wide open.

Pieter negotiates his way across the holes and sides of cracks, balancing Helena in the wheelchair, on the small back wheels. She is a big woman now and he can't lift her.

They cross the road, walking around the potholes, some as big as a duck pond. All the flowers are out. The trees are a vibrant green. The colour in the flowers is extraordinary. The earth quaking has awakened every living thing. There are insects everywhere, and birds flying in and out and around the holes.

Helena is well and truly done. She can't go on. She puts her foot on the ground. Pieter stops. Helena sits in her wheelchair and Pieter sits under a tree. Nothing is as it was. As if he was walking in some other place, some other time. The way time is passing, and the way space is rearranging itself, is unrecognisable, as if he has slipped into another world. Helena's eyes are wide open, her lips never uttering a sound, yet she appears to be taking in every sight, every sound, along the way. Helena's hand squeezes his. He knows that somehow in the midst of all this extraordinariness, someone or something is going to be all right, but he doubts very much it will be them.

As the sun is setting they walk into Princess Margaret Hospital. The lifts are not working. The man at the entrance directs them to two orderlies who carry Helena in the wheelchair up to the first floor. There are people lying in beds and on mattresses everywhere, in the corridors, on the floors, out the doors.

Nurses are going from patient to patient doing their very best. They have food and bottled water, pads and plastic bags. Outside along the front of the building, young men are out placing orange port-a-loos. Pieter settles Helena in as best he can. He checks his cellphone again. Nothing. Hopefully Kay has made her way home by now. He sets off home.

Pou and lacebark, Avon River

6

~Whenua~

Land country
Placenta
Afterbirth

Teihard de Chardin says we are not physical beings having a spiritual journey, but spiritual beings having a physical journey. We are in this place of linear time, this dense place of being.

I watch the graph on the geo-net when an aftershock has occurred. I guess the magnitude, the depth and place and then I watch and wait to see where the epicenter is, and if my guess was right. I always wonder if what I felt was the worst of it, or if the epicentre is somewhere else far away and it is much worse there.

Kara is making her way back across the city, heading for the hills. She looks up across the river. Her son Hemi appears, as if from nowhere. She breathes a sigh of relief. Hemi is alive. Hemi's shirt and jacket and trousers are wonky. He is smoothing his hair and looking around. A tattered camera crew appears.

Kara watches and waits. Hemi looks at his watch. He looks at the sky. The camera folk have got him here, to comment. Hemi clears his throat, brushes dust from his clothes. He takes a bit of concrete in his hair.

"You start Hemi."

Hemi addresses the camera.

"This earthquake you experienced two hours ago is part of a sequence of earthquakes.

The Greendale Fault Sequence began on 4 September 2010, and the Cashel Street Boxing Day earthquake was on 26 December 2010, but this is a different earthquake."

Hemi, "A new fault has been exposed. Some people see lights, or hear a roar before the earthquakes begin, or hear a great boom coming from deep in the earth some minutes afterwards."

Hemi, "This new earthquake fault sequence is centred now in the Cashmere Hills, through and out into Lyttelton Harbour."

"Yes the Greendale fault is still active."

"There could be a tsunami if the earthquakes are centred in the seabed."

"When are the earthquakes going to stop?"

Hemi to the cameras, "We don't know when the earthquakes are going to stop."

"How about an educated guess?"

Hemi, "They could go on for three years, three months, thirty years, thirty months."

"Thirty years? Give us a break, Hemi! We need to reassure people. How could we live like this for thirty years?"

Hemi, "You asked for an educated guess."

Hemi turns back to the cameras, "This is an upward thrusting earthquake that has reverberated back and forth into the city and against the hills. This is a new event distinct from the aftershocks of the first sequence of earthquakes."

The earth shakes. The earth reverberates. They move well away from anything that could fall. They go down on their haunches. They watch the ground. Hemi, "I have to go,"

"What's up ?"

"I have heard nothing from my mother, nor from my brother."

There is another shake. The camera crew disappear. Kara makes her way across the river to Hemi. Hemi sees Kara coming, and meets her on the bridge.

"Hemi!"

"Whaea! You are all right Whaea! Kei hea a Hone?"

"Kua mate a Hone."

Kara and Hemi stand together holding each other on the bridge above the water. Kara has Hone's headband and pounamu in her hands. "Hone is dead. A brick wall in High Street fell on him. I have his shoe. He had one shoe on and one shoe off. Before the tangi, I must go to Hone's place up on Kahukura. "

"I will come with you, Whaea."

Rock crack, Cashmere

7

~Kahu~

Harrier hawk

Foetus membrane

Egg white

Some folk sleep outside through the night, so they aren't running in and out every time there is a shake. Or everyone sleeps together in one room to watch out for each other. The nights are hardest, lying in bed wondering when the next one will come. Half waiting, half trying to sleep, half awake, half asleep. And then when it does come I lie there wondering if it's going to leap up, go on and on, if the books will begin to wobble, the drawers pop out. If it's sharp and big I jump out of bed and get outside well clear of the house.

They come again too. Sometimes huge shakes will follow each other, by an hour, or half an hour, or two or three hours. When the big ones come, we gather together with our neighbours on the street, with our small lights, in our blankets and dressing gowns. Every time a quake comes the house dances on her wooden foundations as if she is doing a Highland fling. I have to get outside.

They say, "Go under the table." When the big ones come, there is no table to go under. The table has been flung across the room. The piano on wheels has whizzed across the floor as if it had a mind of its own.

Pieter is on his bike winding in and out of the potholes. He thinks, surely Kay will have made her way home by now. He makes his way down Barrington Street, to Somerfield Street to his dairy. No one is there. Ti, his Korean assistant has disappeared, probably gone home to see if his family is safe.

Cans, packets, jars, bottles and food are strewn all over the floors. The electricity, the freezers, the lights, the phones, the till are inoperable.

All the provisions have been flung to the floor from the shelves on the east wall of the shop, despite the thin wires Pieter had nailed on, securing them after the first earthquake. Nothing has fallen off the south wall. Things have heaved and jumped to the wire, but they have not made it to the floor.

Pieter throws open the front door of the shop. People arrive, some folk have money, some have no money. Pieter doesn't care. He asks them what they want and gives out baked beans, milk, dates, asparagus, chocolate, spring onions, apples, pears, butter, yoghurt.

Some folk have walked out of the city and have only the clothes they stand up in. He sees the dust in their hair, the faraway look in their eyes. He notices the odd ways they move their limbs as if they aren't attached to their bodies.

Pieter asks a man what he would like.

"Three milk please."

Pieter gives him four plastic bottles and two chocolate fish. The man thanks him with a smile and wanders on his way.

"How can I help?"

"One honey, one cheese, one box of tea please. You see...."

He gives her two honey, one cheese, and two boxes of tea. She gives him a $50 note and waves off any change.

"What would you like?"

"Could I have some water please and some bandages for my Mum. She got glass in her leg."

"Where is she?"

"She is at home. I have taken the glass out of her leg and we have it up. I need a good thick bandage and plasters."

"Is your Mum able to talk and move her other limbs?"

"Yes she can talk and move her legs. She will be all right."

He gives the boy four bottles of water and a first aid kit. The boy gives Pieter two dollars. Pieter waves it off. The boy calls, "Thank you," and runs off down the street.

A man arrives looking absentmindedly everywhere. "What would you like?"

"Yes, yes, I need some food, something to eat."

Pieter sits him down and gives him bread and a banana to eat straight away.

"Something for tea."

"Bread, eggs, baked beans?"

"Yes, yes, I have no electricity and we don't have a fire."

Pieter has two gas burners. He gives one, and a pack of matches to the man.

"Thank you, thank you."

The man gives Pieter two twenty dollar bills, takes the burner, the matches, the bread, the eggs, and the baked beans, and walks off absentmindedly down the road.

Pieter takes food out of the freezer and undamaged cans from the floor and puts them by the door so folk can take whatever they need. People stream in and out. Now and then there is another quake. Pieter and the customers run outside away from the dangling roof and the damaged wall.

The rain comes, and water comes in through the roof. Pieter works on and on, moving stock and food out of the rain. The collapsed wall is in full view and Pieter makes sure the broken roof is not leaking on any perishables. He works on and on until the shop is bare of all perishable food.

Out the back, away from the collapsed building, Pieter secures the small shed as best he can and moves water, food, a table and his bed into the shed. He puts a small gas burner outside on a low rock and sits down and boils water for a cup of tea.

Pieter thinks, Kay should have got here by now, from wherever she was, unless she is helping somebody somewhere. He tries his phone again. It is dead. He looks up to the sky and sees a kahu harrier hawk flying high in the clouds, directly above his shop. The food has all run out of his shop like a river,

Pieter thinks, "Another shake and the whole structure will collapse, but nothing grows rancid, nothing grows old, nothing grows mould, nothing will be left here."

Rock on Hill, Mount Pleasant

8

~Kōtuku~
White heron Feathers

Sacred time, sacred space, beauty, dead autumn leaves, brilliant orange red, rained on, sunned on, tiny trees growing at the side of the track, a still, brilliant, sunny dusk.

When it's your time, you move through out of the dense time filled realm, into the less dense, timeless realm. Out of middle earth, into the celestial realm.

The sky above us stays open, with a twist of your head, it opens and you can see through. These are the openings where folk slip through and into the sky. Those of us left, are living here among these tearings in the fabric of the universe.

Some five minutes after the earthquakes that are centred beneath our feet, under the Cashmere Kahukura area, a huge earth-shattering boom comes. It sounds like rocks falling from a very great height into a great cavern deep inside the earth.

Together Hemi and Kara walk and hitch lifts through the broken city down Colombo Street and up Dyers Pass Road to the sign of the Takahe and then head across the hills to Hone's spot on Kahukura.

Kara is shattered through and through. An age-old weariness descends, envelops, surrounds her, until nothing is recognisable, not anymore. She walks on up the hill as if on instinct. She smells her way. She is a tiny caterpillar sensing her way up the mountain. Shuffling one foot in front of the other, shuffling, can't hold two and three and anything together anymore. All the roads, the fields, the old tracks, are full of mud, unrecognisable. Fudging it, the way back, the way forward. Rivers, everything has become rivers and mud and crevices, everywhere.

Hemi is free. Free from his work, free of the broken city, he runs, bounds, flies across the fallen rocks and on up the hill like a kea. A sudden quake comes, he moves to a sheltered spot and watches the rocks bounce up and out of the ground and down the hill and crash down into the gully below. Then he is on and up again. He gets higher and higher up into the hills, scrambling over boulders, clawing his way on all fours across a track that is now a scree slope. Higher and higher he climbs, all the time looking, careful of rocks falling from above.

Hemi can see clearly now, across the plains, to the mountains of the Southern Alps. He follows the track he and Hone have walked together many times before, touching, feeling the rocks, the trees as he passes, looking about silent, respectful. Another shake comes. He crouches in the shade of an old macrocarpa. He watches in awe as a huge rock bounces up and out of the ground.

The quaking mountain settles and Kara moves out of the shelter. Hemi sees she is weeping. He comes to her and puts his arms around her shoulders. "It's not safe for you here Whaea," he says gently. Kara shakes her head and says nothing. She holds the headband and the pounamu in her hands.

Hemi sits down and puts his head in his hands. Kara goes to him and wraps her arm firmly around his shoulders. She takes his hand gently and places it on the pounamu. His head clears and he sees with clarity, where to go, what to do. Together they walk on and up Kahukura, never stopping or turning back, always scanning the trees, the rocks, the shrubs, the grasses, the sky for a sign.

Kara winds Hone's headband around her wrist. She is walking slowly onward and up the mountains of Kahukura, the red cloak of the sky, of the nor'west arch, and the red rock deep within the Cashmere Hills.

This twilight journey she makes with Hemi among the fleeing and earthquakes and all the haruru. This is to be done for Hone and done now. When they come to an intersection in the tracks, she stays still, closes her eyes and clutches the pounamu and Hone's headband close to her heart.

On and upward they go, higher into Kahukura. When the next quake comes they go to the nearest ngaio and wait there under the tree until the quake passes. Sheltering under the ngaio, they see two huge boulders bounce up and out of the ground like balls. Kara knows they are almost there. There is a soft rainbow in the sky. They follow the rainbow, up and up climbing over the jagged rocks.

They are on the ridge line, they climb through the prickly scrub and get to Hone's place. Kara falls to her knees and buries Hone's headband in the earth, praying karakia for the passing through of Hone.

High on the wind they hear the sound of a kotuku. He comes down and rests not far from where Kara is kneeling. He gazes at Kara and she at him. Hemi stands silent and watchful. The kotuku gazes at Hemi.

"Haere haere haere
Go Hone on the wind
Go through Hone into the light.
To the other place, near, not far away.
Go from this dense physical body realm
Into the less dense, timeless realm.
I love you, I am here for you always,
Whatever form you decide to take.
Go in peace. Haere haere haere."

The kotuku rises and flies up with the wind.

"Slipped through you are, and I have to wear it, walk with it, walk through it, around it. I have to be with you now, how you are, where you are now and accept your actions, your work, your mahi, your being in the other dimension."

Kara bows her acceptance. Hemi gently places his hands on her shoulders and they move on.

Clifton Hill, Sumner

9

~Kahukura~

Rainbow
Red ochre flax cloak
Red nor'west arch
in the sky

The thin, thin veil, here and now, is not much of a veil at all. It is a torn, wide open veil. They say in Donegal the veil is thin. Here the veil is so thin you can disturb the veil merely by blinking an eye.

This wa, this place, this time, here and now, is where it is easy to pass through into the celestial realm. You can fly and wander through walls and be in several places at once and easily wander the planets, the moons, the stars, and the suns. You think of something, some one, some place, some time and you are there.

We are barely walking, more like floating around the city, on the flat, along the riverside, up and around the hills. We are like tattered butterflies, floating on the breeze.

High on the wind Hemi hears the faint sound of a kahu. Kara looks up and sees the kahu circling. She places her hands on her lips, and Hemi is still and silent. They wait and watch. Then they follow the direction of the sound.

Hemi and Kara get up onto the rise and once again they hear on the wind the faint sound of a kahu. Hemi calls the sound of the kahu back to the kahu. Kara looks down at the foot of the ti kouka cabbage tree and sees a woman's blue scarf. She picks up the blue scarf and holds it to her chest. Kara recognises the scarf. She closes her eyes.

Hemi climbs up and around the ledge. Kara's friend Kay is lying on the ledge where she has fallen, a large rock on her leg. Hemi heaves at the rock, then wedges wood under it. He moves it and Kara pulls Kay's leg out. They take Kay into their arms. Kara checks her pulse and shakes her head. Her eyes are full of tears. She cradles Kay, weeping and calling her name again and again. She looks up and sees another large boulder balanced precariously above them. Together they move Kay and themselves out of the way.

They cut harakeke and make a carry platform for Kay out of

the harakeke. Hemi and Kara descend with Kay. They bring Kay down the mountain of Kahukura wrapped in Kara's coat, lying on the harakeke. They bring her home through the tracks down to Hackthorne Road.

Kara is exhausted. Her whole self is awry, rock dust and tiny leaves in her hair. Her jersey is ripped. She looks like she has seen a ghost, not one, not two, but three ghosts, one after the other.

Kara's hair is loose and wild and a bit wet from one of the rains that fell. Her eyes have seen too much death this day. Three men and one woman appear. The men help Hemi. They are carrying the sides of the platform Hemi and Kara made for Kay. They are carrying Kay. The woman is walking beside Kara holding her, singing softly as they walk. Kara doesn't know her or where she is from, she is an angel who has appeared from nowhere by Kara's side.

They make their way down along Hackthorne Road as best they can, around the cracks and wide openings in the road. Pieter is at the door of his empty shop.

Pieter sees them making their way along Barrington Street. He calls out "Kara Kara!" Through her haze, Kara hears him. It is only then that Pieter remembers, Kay had decided to go walking in the hills at lunchtime today. She had taken her running shoes and her track pants. She was in the hills. He walks straight towards them down the centre of the street. His hands outspread, tears streaming down his cheeks. She is gone, slipped through, his beloved, his Kay.

The small group who have come down the hill, stand all together with Pieter and they walk him on home with Kay. Pieter is at the foot of her platform, Hemi and Kara walking with him. They take Kay to the deck at the back of their home.

Pieter sits by Kay. He calls her name softly and he takes her hand in his and he touches her cheek and he kisses her and he wipes the hair from her forehead. He calls her name as if somehow he could call her back into life. He touches all of her beautiful face with his hands. His hands move down her body all the way to her feet gently ever so gently. He bows his head at her feet. He holds her hands in his and he prays, "*Wees egroet Maria vol van genade.* Hail Mary full of grace

De Heer is met U The Lord is with you

Gij zijt de gezegende onder de vrouwen Blessed art thou among women

En gezegend is Jezus de vrucht van Uw schoot.

And Blessed is the fruit of thy womb Jesus

Heilige Maria moeder van God Holy Mary Mother of God

bidt voor ons zondaars Pray for us sinners

Nu en in het uur onze dood Now and at the hour of our death

Amen."

Hemi gets out Pieter's little gas burner. He makes cups of tea and tomato sandwiches. He gets them pieces of chocolate and some raisins from Pieter's broken shop. Then Hemi leaves. He heads across the city to Rehua Marae where Hone is lying. Hemi has Pieter's good bike. It is the quickest way. Kara will follow him as soon as she is warmed and able.

Pieter says, "If Kay had gone for a walk on another day or at another time of the day, she would not have died. If she had waited until the weekend and gone with me on Saturday, as we had planned." Kara says nothing. Pieter goes inside the broken house and shop, and comes out with two blankets and wraps one around Kara. The other he wraps around himself. Kara stays unmoving on the seat watching the flame in the gas burner dancing.

Pieter tells Kara, "She needn't have died, Kara. Kay needn't have died. Why did she go up walking in the hills today of all days? Why was she at that spot at that time?"

Kara is still high up on the mountain with her boy and with Kay.

"They're dead Pieter, all dead."

He takes her hands fresh with flax and dirt, in his two worn hands. "Hone died in my arms in High Street. He had a young man on his shoulders, who was already dead when I arrived there. He had one shoe on and one shoe off. There were broken bricks everywhere. Kay died high up on Kahukura. A huge rock bounced out of the ground and onto her."

Pieter holds Kara's dirt covered hands in his two worn hands, and he prays. Kara closes her eyes and rocks gently to and fro. Pieter gets water, and the women who have arrived prepare Kay's body for laying out. Kara prays karakia.

Blessings on Hone as he passes through
Blessings on Kay as she passes through
Blessings on all of us
Who are left here living in the sunlight among the bones of this quaking city. Amen

Pieter says, "It's not fair, Kara. Kay was not old. She was fine and in the best of health. If only she had come home for lunch."

Kara whispers to Pieter, "If, if, if, forget it. You can't bring her back. I can't bring Hone back." Kara makes ready to leave Kay with Pieter and the women who have arrived at their home.

"I am going to Rehua, Pieter. Hone lies there with the whanau, and Hemi will be there by now. "

"The roads are clogged with cars and many of the roads are broken open and dangerous."

"I am fine. I will walk."

"You are not, Kara. My friend here will take you."

Kara is beyond exhaustion and she simply assents. She climbs into the car and heads through the broken streets away from the falling-down city, through Hagley Park to Rehua Marae, and to Hone, Hemi and the whanau.

Seagull in Cathedral Square

10
~Karoro~
Sea gull
Ribbed venus shell

The earth becomes a sea, the earthsea becomes a roaring, moving beast intelligible only in our most terrifying dreams, our most eloquent nightmares.

The intensity felt in central Christchurch was MM VII. The peak ground acceleration in the heart of Christchurch exceeded 1.8 times the acceleration of gravity (1.8g). The highest recording of 2.2g (MM X plus) was in the Heathcote Valley. This is the highest intensity ever recorded in New Zealand, and one of the greatest ground accelerations ever recorded in the world. In contrast the 2010 Haiti 7.0 earthquake had an estimated peak ground acceleration of 0.5g.

In a corner of the inner city is a great pile of broken rocks. Rescuers have moved from this area and onto the next as they clear through and find who needs help, who can be recovered, and who needs to be got to the hospital, or to the mortuary.

The pile of broken rocks is breathing, barely, only just, breathing. She comes to, Tess, the woman under the rocks, now and then, very slowly. No one knows she is here, no one finds her, or her shoes, or her bag. No one can hear her now.

"I'm never coming out of this hole. I'm staying inside the earth like a mole. Inside here I will adjust, among the daisies and the dust."

There is a small cavity around her head. Her left arm is pinned securely at the shoulder. Her left ankle is caught and twisted.

"Like a small bird in the roots of an old willow,
nobody will come, nobody will find me here."

There's a karoro, a seagull, flying right above her here in the heart of the city. The karoro comes down and lands on the pile of rocks. The rocks are imperceptibly breathing. The karoro stays there after all the people that can flee, have fled, and no more rescuers have come.

There is another aftershock, one of the rocks rolls off the heap where Tess is lying. The karoro flutters up into the air. In the aftershock, Tess's foot and shoulder are pulled and a rock rolls off the heap where Tess is lying. She cries out in pain. Nobody hears her cry.

After the shaking has stopped the karoro flutters down again and settles back on the spot on the rocks above where Tess lies buried. This time the karoro digs a hole out among the dust and the rocks for himself, making a spot in which to settle.

Nobody comes by and disturbs the seagull, but for Hemi who is on Pieter's bike and is biking across the far side of the Square. He notices the karoro return to the spot from where he flew. He sees the karoro clear out a space to settle in among the rocks and dust, and he wonders what the karoro is up to. A karoro can fly anywhere. Why settle here?

Hemi keeps on biking, but he keeps the karoro in his sight. The karoro does not appear to be going anywhere.

Tess is fastened in her underground fortress. Totally pinned, no way out.

"I can be quite comfortable here. I have a shawl. I shall be without fear. I can sleep a long deep sleep. I can't think clearly. I can weep."

Tess is moving in and out of consciousness, and she has become aware of some light, white thing moving very gently, slightly, barely, above her. She hears a faint scratching sound, dust being moved very lightly and then nothing.

Time stands still. Seconds become minutes, minutes become hours. She wonders if the shaking will ever stop. In two seconds it feels as if it has gone on for thirty minutes. It is difficult to hold on to the notion of linear time.

There is another shake. A rock rolls off the pile above Tess, and then there is stillness. With this shake, the karoro rises from his dusty spot, and Hemi jumps off his bike. Tess hears people calling as if from far, far away, to others to get back from a building. Then she looses consciousness. The karoro looks directly at Hemi and squawks at him. Hemi watches the karoro and wonders what the fuss is about.

Tess comes to again, half in and half out of consciousness. "I can stay here quietly with no sound, hiding in this hole in the ground. I didn't start the day like this today. I went to work. It was just an ordinary sort of day."

She begins to doubt if time is real or if it is a figment of her imagination. Time changes in the same way the earth moves like a sea, a road turns into a river. Ever since she came here, it has been like this. Nothing is stable in this place. Nothing can be taken for granted here, ever. She hasn't minded that until now. She wishes she had been some place else when the shaking began this time.

Hemi looks at the hopping karoro and then he copies the karoro. He jumps up and down on one leg on the spot where he was standing. The karoro squawks at the young man again. The karoro hops up and down on one leg, in the same spot above where Tess is lying.

At least, thinks the karoro, I have his attention.

The karoro squawks again at the young man, three piercing squawks, and then he turns his back on the young man and is silent.

Hemi gets back on his bike. He wonders if the karoro is trying to warn him of impending danger. It is a pretty mad thing to be biking through the city in these conditions. A huge quake could occur at any moment.

The karoro flies up and over to where Hemi is, and perches on the handlebar of Hemi's bike. The karoro looks directly at Hemi, squawks and then hops his way from Hemi, across the Square, to his dusty spot on the rocks above Tess. Hemi watches the karoro. He follows the karoro and heads across the Square to the spot where the karoro has been sitting.

Tess is now moving in and out of consciousness. She sings very softly to herself, "I guess they think we are all dead. I guess it's over now but I am scared. I can't hear anyone cry. I wonder how long it takes to die."

The young man is just above her. He hears something very soft, as if someone is singing a long way off, very quietly. He hears the singing inside his head. The karoro doesn't fly away when Hemi comes near, but stays his ground and looks directly at Hemi.

Hemi sits down on the rocks. The karoro digs with his foot at the dust and rock as if making a better nesting spot. Hemi copies the karoro. He removes a rock, then another, then another. The karoro flies up into the air and hovers above the young man. He looks at the seagull. The karoro looks at him. And then he hears her quiet voice again, as if she is inside his head.

"It doesn't matter if I die like a snail, if I slip quietly through the veil. It's a simple way to die. To be hit by a rock and then to fly."

It is as if he can hear her thoughts. He looks at the karoro and then he knows, the karoro can hear the same thoughts he can hear.

"Anybody there? Anybody there?"

He calls out, but no sound comes back. He listens inside his head again.

"I can smell smoke burning. Where is the smoke coming from?"

This time the young man asks without speaking, inside his own head,

"Where are you?"

"I am lying here pinned by my right shoulder in the rocks under your feet."

The karoro flies up and onto a lamp post above the rocks. The karoro sits waiting, watching, a guardian bird. Hemi removes the rocks one by one from beneath his feet. Hemi asks inside his head, "Am I getting closer?"

"Move to the left and then straight down. Take care with the rocks, I am not far below you. I can smell smoke. Where is the smoke coming from?"

Hemi can smell smoke too. He doesn't know where it is coming from. He just knows that he has to dig and dig quickly to her, to the voice he can hear inside his head.

He finds her right foot first and then her right arm and hand. She does not respond at all, but he can feel her pulse faintly. On and on he digs.

Two others come over and help with the last of the rocks and then, together with Hemi, they shift the huge beam that is lying across her left side. As they lift the beam, Hemi sees the karoro fly up from the lamp post and into the air. Then the karoro is gone.

At one stage in the lifting she opens her eyes and she sees Hemi, she looks into his eyes, then she is gone again. The men lift her out of the hole and they carry her to a stretcher and the others walk her on the stretcher through the broken streets to the hospital.

Hemi stands there bereft, barely moving, unable to resume any work. The karoro is gone. The young woman's soft voice inside his head is gone. He doubts she will survive. He finds his shovel and goes back over to the hole where he was working. But he has no heart for it. He sits at the edge of the hole, his head in his hands, weeping.

II

Anglican Cathedral, Square

11

~Kūwaha~

Gateway

Entrance

Mouth

There have been no shakes since 9 pm last night, when a 4.1 centred in the Heathcote Valley, shook round the hills, I thought it was a 4.2. There are odd holes in the streets, some small, some as big as a house, and all through the streets are rugged cracks and tracks with volcanic silt coming up through the cracks.

In the inner city, hundreds of buildings are wrecked. The CTV building failed and pancaked to the ground during the 22 February 2011 quake, despite the care taken in writing and implementing New Zealand's earthquake building standards over many years following the 1931 Napier earthquake. Many of the people who died in the quake, were in the CTV building. You asked for photos. I can't do that yet, feels like taking photos of a gaping wound, mine own, bloodied and open to the sky.

There are not that many people moving around in the inner city now. The rescuers and emergency services are clearing folk out and checking for anyone who is still trapped. The camera crew can't see Hemi immediately. He is not in the spot where they agreed to meet. Hemi can see the two cameramen there, waiting.

The shaking during the first night of aftershocks woke him five times. It is like that each night. He goes outside and sits on the armchair in the garden, his earthquake chair, away from the buildings and the great trees and watches the moon. But the distant boom of huge rocks falling inside the earth, which comes later, some minutes after the shake itself, chills him to the bone wherever he is.

Hemi wipes the tears from his eyes, straightens his jacket, brushes the dust off his trousers, and prepares himself. He picks up pieces of small rock, bits of wood, and glass off the ground as if somehow this will make sense of it all, and he tries desperately to calm himself.

Hemi can't think of anything to say to them. Who would want

to be talking to the press today? Who would want to know? But he knows the people need to hear a voice, a voice of calm, even if it is out of the wreckage of his own life. They look to him. He is a geologist, who knows. He has studied earthquakes. He is an expert from the University. He decides he will do it.

"We'll put it off until tomorrow."

"No, everyone is broken here, all of us. There needs to be a voice of calm."

"You don't need to do it today."

"I can do it. Hone will help me. I am here to do it."

Hemi bends down and picks up a piece of rock in his hands. He holds it, and rubs, smoothing it with his fingers. He tries carefully to settle himself with the piece of broken rock. He is making sense of it all with his hands, his body, his fingers rubbing the rock. After a while he looks up.

"If you want to."

"I am ready."

"Are you sure you want to?"

They walk slowly over to the spot. An acrid smell of smoke blows into the Square. Hemi sniffs and rubs his nose to wipe the smell away. The smell doesn't leave. He motions to the cameraman to move to the other side of the Square. There is another shake. Where they are standing, the ground opens. They move sideways to another spot. The ground is uneven, the hole is wide and deep, the edges jagged, bigger than a car. Eventually the quake subsides. They begin.

Hemi, "The largest earthquake we experienced was on 4 September 2010. Since then all of the earthquakes have been decreasing in size, although there are blips when the magnitude pops up again, but not so high as that first one."

"Some of the more recent earthquakes have been shallower, closer to the city centre, more damaging, many more people have been injured and killed. The 22 February 2011 earthquake is a new event. It is the beginning of a new sequence of aftershocks."

"We don't know. We don't know if other earthquake events will occur and open up a further sequence of aftershocks. In this case they could go on for days, weeks, months, or years.""

"Thirty years? "

"Maybe," says Hemi.

There is another tremor. The camera crew and Hemi all crouch down and wait it out.

Hemi, "This is a deep, long, rolling motion, rocking from side to side, earthquake. It is characteristic of the Rolleston fault."

"The ones that are centred under the Cashmere Hills?"

Hemi, "The ones centred under the Cashmere Hills are sharp jolting upward thrusting earthquakes. Most earthquakes occur where the tectonic plates are colliding. In the case of the Christchurch earthquakes, the tectonic plates are splitting."

"Inside the central four avenues of the city has been cordoned off by the army. The buildings in this densely built up area, are dangerous and could fall and injure more people in subsequent earthquakes."

"The Cathedral in the Square is badly damaged. The Cathedral War Memorial statue of the Woman with the Angel wings curving the sword into a bow above her head, the Chalice and the Cairn of Waimakariri river stones, are intact. Robert Godley has fallen over and broken. The tramlines are twisted. All of the buildings within the four Avenues are damaged and being assessed."

"Please keep warm and drink water. There are halls and marae to go to for shelter, or move in with relations or friends if your places are too badly damaged. There are cheap flights out of the city and there are places to stay throughout the South Island with food and free accommodation if you are able to travel.

We have ordered thousands of port-a-loos to be delivered into the city. Milk tankers will be bringing truckloads of water into the city. Depots are being set up and you can collect water from these depots. Use any fuel you have sparingly. Keep dry and stay warm and check in with all of your neighbours."

As they head off, Hemi gives each of the crew a hongi and a warm hug. Then he sits down on a rock at the edge of a hole, shattered. Hone died in High Street. Kay died up on Kahukura. He wonders what happened to the girl he pulled out of the rubble. Where will she be buried? Who are her family? Where are they living? He would like to tell them he was with her.

He knows he can't bring Hone back no matter what he does, and now there is this girl whom he never knew, who could talk with him inside his head, even when she was buried under the rubble. She stays with him. He can't get her out of his mind.

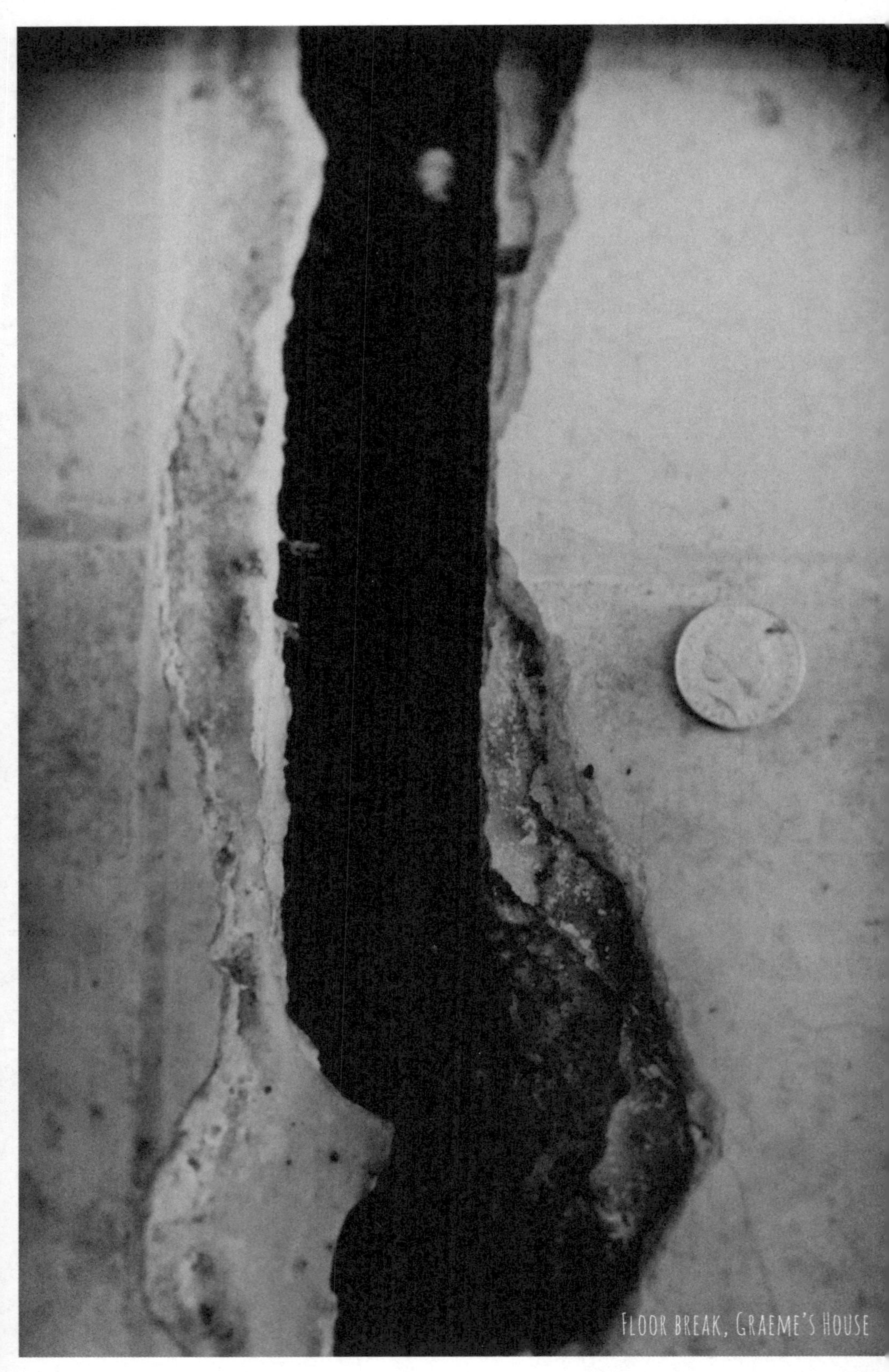
Floor break, Graeme's House

12

~Taniwha~

Fabulous monster
Awesome one
Water spirit

The brilliant yellow orange tips of the leaves of the ti kouka cabbage tree, are shining in the sunlight. The leaves of the ti kouka cabbage tree are flexing and breathing into the wind. The ti kouka is full of tiny white flowers dancing in the light breeze. Her tiny flowers glittering, twinkling like stars. Sparkling true like a shining star, true to the joy, true to the pain.

Deep grey black clouds and the odd white one drift in a transparent blue sky. Sunlight is soft on the soul, soft on the faces, on all the places, all of the people, whom I am burying with my own heart, my own hands.

Broken open apart, not whole anymore. Hua i a koe! Name yourself! How do we name ourselves, birth ourselves, in this place, in this time? Stay with the joy, the pain. Stay true to the pain and the joy. Hua i a koe — Name yourself, birth yourself.

The deep black piwakawaka came again today. Kara only hopes and prays it is for Hone and Kay and no more. They make their way by car around the park. Hemi looks up and sees Kara, his own mother in a car by the river. She is looking everywhere, and nowhere. Hemi calls out to them. They slow and stop. Hemi runs over to Kara. "Kia ora Whaea,"

"Haere mai e Tama." They hongi. Kara holds him and he buries his head in her breast.

"This seagull, a karoro took me to these rocks. I dug this hole in the rubble and there was this beautiful kotiro, but she was barely breathing. They took her to the hospital."

Kara holds Hemi, "Your aunties and cousins are preparing Hone now as we speak. Hone is being taken to Koukourarata at dusk." Hemi looks around at the broken buildings and the rescuers and then up at the sky.

He gets in with Kara and they move slowly along beside split open, partly falling buildings, past the trees still standing as if nothing had happened, along Bealey Ave, where the big brick homes of yesteryear have their chimneys fallen through, their walls askew.

They get to Rehua Marae and find Hone in the casket, wrapped in his feather cloak. With the aunties, uncles, and cousins all together and with the others following, they make their way with Hone in the hearse, through and out of the broken city over the quaking hills through Governors Bay, Diamond Harbour to Koukourarata, Port Levy.

Hone lies at the beautiful marae of Koukourarata, above the sea. Everyone is helping in large and small ways, preparing kai, laying the hangi. A few guys are out in the boats catching fish. Tara lights the candles around Hone in his casket. Folk come and go, saying their farewells to a good son, a brother, a cousin, a friend, a nephew, a work mate, talking, laughing, praying and singing through the three long summer days and nights.

People walk along beside the water. Then through the hills, following Hemi and his uncles and his cousins carrying Hone up the hill, singing waiata, consoling each other, weeping as they walk. They are sending Hone safely on his journey through the heavens. Ensuring that his passage through is not fraught, that he can move swiftly on his way. Kara and her sisters pray, sing and karanga Hone, as he goes on his way,

"*Kake ake ki te Pumotomoto* Ascend to Pumotomoto
O Tikitiki-o-rangi The entrance to Tikitiki-o-rangi
I Tawhiri-rangi And to Tawhiri-rangi
O Te Toi-o-nga-rangi-tuhaha In Te Toi-o-nga-rangi-tuhaha.

Kara sits still on the hill above Koukourarata. The wind is settling down. Kara watches the sun setting, the sky turn orange, red, burning gold. A kotuku, a white heron, makes his way soundlessly across the hills. The wind flutters her cloak now and then. She has a pounamu in her hand over her heart. She moves her fingers across its surface as if unaware that she is moving her hands.

Kara wants to crawl into the ground, stay there and never come out. She opens her mouth to speak, but no sound comes. She opens her mouth wide. The wind flows in. She breathes in the wind. The thin high sound comes out like a weeping from deep inside her. She sees the kotuku high up above her calling on the wind.

The kotuku flies close over her head. She recognises him. Her eyes fill with tears and she weeps. The kotuku sits on the rock near her. Then a deep peace fills her. The kotuku is very beautiful, she tells him so.

"I wish you were here beside me, in your young man's body, Hone."

He tells her, "Otautahi is where the first season comes. Christchurch, Aedes Christus, is the home of Christ consciousness. Change is coming through, heralded by the earthquakes. This place is a birthing canal. One of the places on earth where the old breaks down and the new emerges."

Kara argues with him, "But why have you passed through? You could be here."

He replies, "We are to work together, Whaea, across the dimensions."

Kara looks up into the sky, the moon is on her way up, the first stars are appearing. Kara looks far out to sea. The kotuku disappears into the night.

Kara sees Hemi trudging up the hill towards her. He reaches her. They hongi. Kara goes with Hemi. Together they walk down the hill to Koukourarata.

Tuawera Cave Rock hollow

13

~Puare~

Hole, hollow
Be exposed
Opening

Big earthquakes, wakes, tangihanga and funerals come in waves. From every direction, dressed in black, hundreds of people walk together to churches, to marae, to homes, to funeral places, to cemeteries, praying, singing, talking, walking, to farewell our loved ones. Walking eases the pain. It helps us, the living, to move with the pain.

Old trees hold memories of the earthquakes inside their rings. I feel like an old tree holding memories of the earthquakes inside my rings. There is a hole in me as big as the sky. It goes out from my body and embraces trees, grass, broken buildings, flowers, birds, water, mud, and tar. It embraces the broken streets full of strange shapes drawn in the ground, birds and insects flying above the ground, herbs, weeds and flowers growing in the ground. The hole is wide and open. It is the colour of soft olive green, not the underside, but the colour of the top of a feijoa, or of an olive leaf. Today the hole permeates me inside out, upside down.

Grey clouds are drifting across the sky from the mountains. There is snow hiding inside the grey cloud. The window of the soul, the way through, is the colour of feijoa and olive. We eat feijoa when it falls from the tree, only in winter. We eat olive only after it has been brined and sat for weeks or months. Brined, or falling from the tree the colour is the same, soft olive green.

Kara is at home. She doesn't wish to go anywhere at all. She meditates, she contemplates, she talks to herself, trying to unravel the earthquakes and all that has happened. She wants to lie on the side of the hill under the snakeskin gum, curled in a ball and weep her way through the day. Today she can't see the stunning white snow mountains. They are covered in low grey misty cloud as if they were not there at all. She wonders how people get up and do ordinary things, eat their breakfast, read the paper, ride their bike, and go to work, on a day like this.

She sees them slipping through, before her very eyes, her loved ones, her beloved. Those who cared for her, ran the bath for her, fed her when she was a babe, cuddled her, held her tight. She sees them all slipping through. There is no way she can call them back. Except when they come unbidden and speak with her by her side. They are become now of the wairua, the spirit.

Today she stays with, and pays homage to them. Inch by inch, she plants her gardens for them. She plants gardens of flowers and fine herbs and trees, makes sandy birdbaths, and plants apple trees for birds to feed on, in winter. She makes places to touch rock and stone, to stand barefooted, and to be embraced by the earth.

On a day like this, there is no place else to be but in the garden, in bare feet, the earth in her toes, beneath the sky.

Blessings of light
on this sacred part of your journey
Be in God, of God, one with God
on this sacred part of your journey
May God hold you in the palm of hand
on this sacred part of your journey
May God be with you and bless you
on this sacred part of your journey
Love and blessings of holiness and light
on this sacred part of your journey.

High Street

14

~Moe~

Sleep, sleep with Dream Beget

Last night I went to bed. I slept all night like a baby. No quakes woke or disturbed me. I dreamed of things the way they were before the earthquakes. When I awoke I thought everything was back how it was before. The wind was blowing the leaves on the flowering snakeskin gum. A butterfly was drifting on the breeze. Sunlight was streaming in the window above my bed. Nobody had died. Nothing was broken. The world felt good and whole.

I looked out the other window and saw the house on the hill across the valley. The whole front of the big brick house was sheared off and large pieces were lying all over the ground. I was waking out of my dreamtime, into a nightmare.

Four days after the 22 February quakes begin, just as we are running out of our supplies of water, the Council organises milk tankers of water from South Canterbury for the city. Folk queue up to fill bottles and containers with water from milk tankers filled with water, not milk.

I like open spaces and trees and walking by water. The destruction is not from a war, from other people fighting us. It is our earth Papatuanuku attacking the buildings, the things that people have created on her surface.

Maybe Papatuanuku is not so fussed on tall pointy spires, big rectangle buildings, roads, tar pavements, concrete foundations, stone, brick structures we have created. She is gentler on the wooden structures and on curving buildings. The ones that sway, move, creak and groan, but don't break or crumble.

Pieter gets to the funeral place and there are people everywhere. One of the buildings is unusable. There is a queue of people. He can't bear it. So he leaves and walks home.

He has Kay at home, laid out on a beautiful red velvet cloth, with flowers all around her. She looks as if she were sleeping. He kisses her forehead, but it is cold. He holds her hand, but her hand is still and cold. She feels as if she is near, but not in her body anymore.

Hemi comes by to pay his respects. He has a big bunch of wild flowers. Pieter has never seen big strong Hemi with a bunch of flowers. He smiles and takes the flowers and places them near Kay.

"There are no caskets ready."

"We'll make one for Kay," says Hemi. "I can find some wood. I have the workshop."

Pieter and Hemi go down the road to Hemi's workshop, away from where Kay lies with her family and friends gathered round. Together Pieter and Hemi cut the wood, curve it. They drill holes in the wood and they stitch the sides and base together with blue rope and make a white pine casket for Kay, and Hemi carves her name, Kay, out of wood and places it on the casket.

Friends, family, workmates and old school mates gather together with Pieter and they walk together with Kay in her beautiful casket down Simeon Street singing her on her way to the wooden Sacred Heart Church in Addington.

At the Mass, the people gather to walk up together to receive communion and the blessing. Pieter doesn't cry. Pieter is brave and he speaks of the time he first met Kay and of her beauty and of her love of the mountains and the wild high places.

WATER ROCK, ESTUARY

15

~Puna~

Well, pool
Spring of water
To well up, flow

In Dallington the river turns off its old course and runs deep down the whole street. A spring pops up in the middle of someone's living room. Another spring opens in the middle of a road. A huge boulder rolls down the hill and lands on a toilet in Mount Pleasant crushing the seat into little pieces.

Everywhere springs pop up. The Press *newspaper declares we are now a city of ten thousand springs. All the old underground springs, the swampland breathing, the birds and ducks returning in droves, everywhere.*

Three days after the big one the south and east of the city begin to run out of water. It isn't that we haven't put aside lots of water for an emergency. It is just that lots of other folk haven't put any water aside. We share our water with the others in the neighbourhood who have run out.

Pieter makes his way to Princess Margaret Hospital and Helena. When he gets there he see two rows of port-a-loos standing outside like sentinels in front of the hospital. He finds Helena in the half-light, half standing with the aid of her walking frame. She is very unstable.

He goes inside and packs up her few belongings very quickly. He talks gently to Helena, and he guides her and they head out of the hospital.

Tess is walking out of the hospital on her crutches. She walks straight into Pieter and Helena. Tess can't walk very well but she can balance on her crutches. Her head is muddled too, her thinking muddied. She is making her way across the city. She has discharged herself from the hospital. There are people in there worse off than she and she can't bear to be in there on the fifth floor when the building is shaking. It brings it all back. She remembers how it was under the rocks and is terrified.

She knows that even the hospital building could collapse just like the one she was in, in the city and she isn't going to be in there, if it happens. She is bandaged up and she manages to get some crutches and then she leaves the hospital. She has been unable to contact anyone else in the city. Her phone is dead and buried. She thinks her parents, who live in Guangzhou, may know of the earthquakes by now and be worried. She will contact them today.

Pieter has his head down and is watching his feet and Helena's walking frame negotiate the steps to the entranceway and onto the street. He walks straight into Tess.

He looks up. "I'm sorry," he says.

And then he looks again, as if he recognises Tess from somewhere.

"You were in town?"

"I was in town," Tess says evenly.

"Were you in the centre of the city during the quake?" Tess makes her way with Pieter and Helena along the bumpy, potholed street to his place, walking, there is no other way. Helena sings softly, "*Stille nacht heilige nacht* Silent night, holy night."

Pieter joins in with Helena, "*Alles slaapt sluimert zacht* All is calm all is bright."

He smiles at Helena and hugs her. They plod on around the long curvy open road, around the big potholes and the little dips and cracks.

"*Eenzaam waakt het hoogheilige paar* Round yon virgin mother and child
Lieflijk Kindje met goud in het haar Holy infant so tender and mild
Sluimert in hemelse rust Sleep in heavenly peace
Sluimert in hemelse rust Sleep in heavenly peace."

Tess walks quietly beside them.

Pieter asks, "Where are you from?'

"I am from Guangzhou."

"Guangzhou?"

"In the South of China."

"Where were you?"

"No one was left where I was."

"Where were you?"

Tess says nothing.

"Everyone else had gone, or ..."

" Near the Square?"

Tess nods.

Tess says quietly, "I was buried under the rubble."

"You are lucky to be alive."

"I am."

"A young man removed the rocks and he got me out. "

"He dug you out of the rubble?"

Tess nods.

Pieter says nothing. He just walks on beside Tess, with Helena by his side.

Helena sings quietly to herself to calm herself, "*Stille nacht heilige nacht* Silent night, holy night.

Pieter joins in with Helena,

Alles slaapt sluimert zacht All is calm all is bright..."

"He found you?"

"It was strange that he found me."

Tess scratches her head.

"When he was digging above me, it was like he could read my mind. If there had been a big enough shake when he was in there, anything could have happened."

"He risked his life for you? "

Tess nods.

A big shake comes. Tess goes pale. She leans her body against a tree. Pieter holds tightly to Helena, lest she fall. He puts out a hand towards Tess. Tess takes his hand. The shaking subsides.

"Good to meet you. I am Pieter."

"I am Tess."

"You are welcome to eat dinner tonight with us."

Pieter says to Helena, "We will have a good dinner, Helena." Helena nods. Pieter wonders how on earth he is going to care for Helena. He has only a little outside shed still standing and he is not even sure if that is safe. He can dig out a long drop somehow somewhere a bit away from the little shed. The shop where he lives and works is too unsafe. No one can sleep in the shop, but he can get things out of there. Everything is awry. He can't settle anything down in his mind.

Out of the blue Tess says, "I can't walk properly. I can't think straight."

"You are alive."

"I am."

"Your back is not broken."

"It is not."

"You can walk."

"I can hobble."

"Where is your house?"

"The place where I lived is inside the red zone. I have no cash, no money, no food, no cards. It is all buried. No job. The place where I worked is buried under rubble and inside the red zone. No clothes. Only what I stand up in."

"It could be worse."

"I could be dead."

"You can get along on those crutches."

"I can hop."

"My shop is broken in half. I can use one side, but it is cold and the rain gets in. There is no running water."

Tess spots a plum tree. "I can balance on one crutch and pick plums from that tree."

"All the electricity is off. I have a gas burner, we can cook tea on the burner."

Helena singing quietly on," *Sluimert in hemelse rust* Sleep in heavenly peace

Sluimert in hemelse rust Sleep in heavenly peace."

They walk on the three of them together along the broken opened pavement.

They sit down on a fence to rest.

Tess says "I must contact my parents and tell them I am fine. I don't want them to worry."

They get up and wander on down the road. The light is fading. A full moon is coming out as they make their way into the backyard of Pieter's broken shop. He carts the bed out of the broken shop and into the shed and sets Helena up on the bed and settles Helena.

Around the back he has dug a hole and put on a toilet seat, and covered it around with corrugated iron. There is no roof. It is open to the stars. "You can sit here, Mama, watch the sky, watch the patches of rain come and go, and the clouds drift by."

At the edge of Pieter's yard, near the street, a steady stream of water is bubbling up. It is good clear water. He has placed a tub to catch the spring water for their use. The rest of the water overflows and goes across the pavement and down the gutter. "I found a spring Mama, just near the gate. Beautiful clear spring water, here, sip it. They said springs opened up during the earthquakes. The old springs that used to be here!"

Tess gets water from the spring. She boils the water and makes them all a cup of tea. Then she opens a large tin of baked beans and cooks the beans in a pot on the gas burner. Pieter brings out some bread.

As the evening goes on, folk queue up with buckets and bottles and stand at the spring near Pieter's gate — fresh, clear water. Folk walk or bike to collect water from the well in bottles and containers. They chat and share stories and walk and bike and queue together. They have water, even if it means walking or biking to the spring each morning and carrying the water home in their bottles, on their bikes. When the water comes on tap again, some folk keep collecting pure spring water from the well.

Cenotaph, Cathedral Square

16

~Mārama~

Moon

Month

Light, clear

I become alert to the full moons, the new moons, to the moon perigee, to the waxing of the moon, the waning of the moon, to the winter and summer solstice, to the spring and autumn equinoxal winds. I follow the moon when she rises and sets with the sun at new moon, and when she rises and sets with the stars, at full moon. The days are warm, still, hot, dry, sunny days. Earthquake weather, my Nana used to say. It goes on and on and on, this earthquake weather, raining often everywhere in the country, but not here, where the earthquake vibrations continue to pour through.

I check National Institute of Weather and Atmosphere (NIWA) reports for the high risk, dangerous times at sea and they are the same for us on land with the earthquakes. Things are pretty active around those times. I never go up on a roof around the time of the new or full moon and when the moon is closest to the earth at the perigee.

Hemi is walking around the city in his yellow hard hat and orange vest, taking geological notes, trying to make sense of what has happened. "Most of the trees survived. The statues of the men all fell flat on their faces. All of the men fell, except Captain James Cook, the navigator, in Victoria Square. They began building St Michael's in stone. There were earthquakes in Christchurch from 1869 all through 1870, for eighteen months, while they were building St Michael's, so they changed and built St Michael's in wood. The Cathedral in the Square was designed to be in wood. An English Anglican Bishop turned up and had it built in stone. An old, very dangerous European commitment to stone, the locals only built in wood and raupo.

Warm, hot, sunny, windless, stunning weather, normally we would be lying out at the beach surfing and bodysurfing the waves, digging sandcastles and moats and rivers, lying on the sand, enjoying the sun.

In the central city only two churches have survived intact,

Catholic St Mary's and Anglican St Michael's. The Mary line and the Michael line are old sacred dowsing lines that run through the St Mary's and St Michael's churches of Europe. The woman curving a sword in her hands in the sky, on the cenotaph, in the Square, is intact. The chalice sculpture of leaves whirling in the Square, is intact.

The cairn of river stones, is also intact. Orders had been made for the cairn of river stones to be dismantled on 24 February two days after the 22 February earthquake happened. It is still standing.

An odd piece in the newspaper this morning, seismic testing for oil by the Andarko research vessel *Aquila* began on 22 February and a day or two later *The Press* reports *Aquila* limps damaged into Lyttelton harbour. No information on what damaged the *Aquila*.

Seismic testing for oil and gas was rushed through Parliament and approved for the Canterbury basin four hours after the 22 February earthquake. All the Canterbury MPs had left the House for Christchurch. Were they doing seismic testing on the *Aquila* when the quake happened?

Hemi makes his way across the broken Square to talk in front of the cameras. The ground shakes beneath them. The cameras shake, they all shake. Strange earthquake descriptions go through Hemi's mind. "This is a rocking-from-side-to-side-lightning-bolt of an earthquake. This is a jeep-turning-on-its-side-sinking-slowly earthquake. This is a house-dancing-on-its-poles earthquake. This is a building-collapsing-like-a-sandwich earthquake!"

The quaking subsides. The camera folk pack up and leave.

Hemi sits there in the Square, in his hard hat and his orange vest looking at the woman on the cenotaph making the sword into a curve between her two hands high in the sky. He wonders how she survived. She stands for peace, he thinks, that Woman Holding A Curving Sword above her head, beside the Anglican Cathedral.

He walks over to the spot where he dug out the girl buried in the pile of rocks, and he sits there. He wonders where she is, how she is doing in the heavens.

Rapanui Shag Rock

17

~Tara~

Pre-dawn light
White fronted Tern
Moon wane
Vagina, Peak

One hundred and eighty nine people were killed on the day of the February earthquake but hundreds more have since perished from common illnesses, accidents, cancers, heart attacks and unusual diseases of the mind and body that no one can diagnose.

The constant trauma is reactivated thousands of times over. The trauma is deep inside our tissues, deep inside our bones. Many of us have no idea of the long lasting effects on our psyche and our bodies from the earthquakes. It gets so deep inside, that's it's hard to ever get it out. It manifests itself in shingles, rickets, skin infections, back pain, joint pain, mania, psychosis, neuralgia, flu, pneumonia, anxiety, lung infection, heart failure, delusions, hallucinations, strokes, indigestion, kidney and liver failure, premature cancers.

We become ill, vulnerable to accidents, so busy are we assisting with the external rebuild, we forget our own internal brokenness. We forget the need for our own internal rebuild.

At night Kara walks along Sumner beach. The sun is setting, a thin shaft of moon rising. The huge cliffs above the beach have broken houses falling down their flanks and resting among rocks and debris. When a quake comes, the birds fly in groups up and into the air. The birds haven't found their new nesting places.

The cliff line is ragged and bare. When the next quake comes, the cliffs break and fall, the dust rises, smoking the air. The cliffs make huge booming sounds as they fall. The booming echoes, right through her, through the earth, and then deep down from way inside the earth another boom comes as if answering.

She sits and meditates, by Rapanui Shag Rock, the only place other than Easter Island in the whole of the Pacific, to be named Rapanui. This is where the great rock face carving peoples of Easter Island came. They used all of their resources to carve the great beings out of rock and left nothing for themselves to live on. Rapanui does not resemble and is no longer the shape of a prow of a great petrified waka. Rapanui is no longer the big sternpost of the waka, neither anymore is it an ure, a penis thrusting upward to the sky. It is hollowed out, become a vessel, a shelter, an opening.

Kara watches the sky turn mauve and red. She hears the seabirds calling — the black backed gulls, the karoro, the black fronted terns, the oyster catchers, the grey white seagulls. Two mollyhawks call and drop pipi and cockles from a great height in the sky onto the sand to split open so they can eat their kaimoana. She walks along the edge of the sand, in her bare feet, wandering in and out of the seawater. Every so often a big wave comes in and washes over her legs, splashing her trousers. She doesn't care. Maybe if she sits here quiet and bare it will all stop. She climbs up on a rock behind Rapanui. She's not cold. She sits still and bare, under the stars.

They have all passed through. Yet here she is, in her body. They could be here, walking the beach, with her. She hears a movement in the waves, she looks up in the moonlight and see an aihe, a dolphin, jump up out of the water, turn a pirouette, just beside the broken open Rapanui, Shag Rock, and then disappear into the ocean.

Rapanui the rock has been split open as if by a bolt of lightning. The top half is in pieces, the faces around the sides are broken and fallen into the water. Rapanui has become a new being, revealing a new face, Te Kou o Te Tara. Tonight the water swirls all around her. Marking the shifting, the change, the birthing, the time when the feminine reveals herself, the becoming, the coming of the time of the Whaea o te Ao, the Mother of the World.

Catholic Cathedral Angels

18

~Whakaoho~

Startle
Awaken
Arouse

Over the next ten days rumours surface around the city, that Mary, Mother of Jesus, appeared high in the left turret of the broken Cathedral, facing out over the city, during the earthquakes. The right turret of the Cathedral was destroyed but the left turret only partly damaged.

On the tenth day The Press, *on the front cover page, prints a huge photo of Mary standing in the left turret of the Catholic Cathedral, behind the broken glass of the window. The cathedral bell ringers come forward. They say they had placed a statue of Mary in the left turret of the cathedral, facing inwards. That is why no one had ever seen her there before. On the 22 February at 12.51pm, when the earthquake occurred, the right turret fell down, but the turret where Mary stood, remained, and the statue of Mary turned 180 degrees and faced out directly over the people of the City of Otautahi Christchurch.*

The Russian Orthodox say Mary has been known to do this in the past — to turn and save sailors, and to stop storms and earthquakes. If the quake had gone on for a few seconds longer, thousands, not hundreds, of people would have perished. Some weeks later, Mary is taken to the Carmelites and then to the Catholic Pro-Cathedral, St Mary's in Manchester St where she stands surrounded by lighted candles to this day.

Reality is sprinkled with broken bones, broken houses, broken jobs, broken people, broken everything and yet some things remain standing. We continually see what would before have been unimaginable things.

We are walking a tightrope beneath the stars, half alive, half dead, raw, empty, opened wide. We are overawed, taken utterly by surprise. Our decisions change. The way we view things is irrevocably altered.

We are broken like in a war, except it is not a war. We are traumatised as people are in a war zone, yet we do not become fearful of other people. We have more faith and trust in other people than ever before. We are fearful of the earth opening and of brick walls, of shop facades and rocks, of chimneys and lifts and skyscrapers falling. There are more insects and birds everywhere. Flocks of birds where there was one or two.

Pieter is making his way home. He is walking along Barbadoes Street in front of the Catholic Basilica. One of the turrets is broken and fallen down. The centre tablet, held aloft by two angels, is intact. "Tabernaculum Dei", Tent of God, is written in the white stone held high in the air. In the left turret, the one still intact, Mary stands, facing over the city.

Pieter does a double take. He has never seen Our Lady standing high in the turret before. Both of the turrets have always been blank, just clear glass. He screws up his eyes and looks again, wondering if his eyes are playing tricks on him. He shuts his eyes and opens them, shuts and opens them, but Our Lady is standing there, looking out over the city.

Pieter goes down on his knees and he prays, "*Wees egroet Maria vol van genade.* Hail Mary full of grace

De Heer is met U The Lord is with you

Gij zijt de gezegende onder de vrouwen Blessed art thou among women

En gezegend is Jezus de vrucht van Uw schoot.

And Blessed is the fruit of thy womb Jesus

Heilige Maria moeder van God Holy Mary Mother of God

Bidt voor ons zondaars Pray for us sinners

Nu en in het uur onze dood Now and at the hour of our death

Amen."

Pieter gets up from his knees, Our Lady is still there. She has two angels to the right, above her head, carved in white stone, and bits of building fallen around her. She is looking out from the broken Cathedral of the Blessed Sacrament, over the ripped streets, over the buildings and the people.

Pieter says, "Mary, Mother of God, you are there among it all, all serene. What are you doing here in these ruins? Among all this death and destruction? You come here?

My wife Kay — please help her on her way through the heavens. And I have a serious problem Mary. My mother, Helena, is away with the fairies and Nazareth House, where she was staying, is destroyed with liquefaction and broken pipes in the ceilings.

I took Helena to Princess Margaret Hospital, but there is no water there, no sewerage, only port-a-loos, but they have pads. She is in shock and she doesn't understand the earth quaking on and on and on and on. So I brought her home and now she is with me, and I have no electricity and a broken down house."

There is a big shake. Pieter moves further back from the Cathedral. The side of the cathedral cracks open, further away from the huge domes. Our Lady stays where she is.

Pieter takes one last look at her, he genuflects before Our Lady. He blesses himself, then he waves her goodbye.

Crack with Twig, Estuary

19

~Tūrangawaewae~

Place of belonging

Some folk born and bred here who are living on the other side of the world or other parts of the country are affected, as if the shaking of the earth has also gone inside their bones. This place is their turangawaewae, the place they call home. For these folk this place is indelible in them and is unutterably altered. The earth not flat, stable, not hard, solid, a rock on which to perch to hold fast, but a living breathing ocean of an earth Papatuanuku. This is her nature and now and then for a few decades or more we are lulled to sleep in the bosom of a still calm ocean.

Some folk living overseas raise money to help and support us here. Some simply pack up wherever they are and shift home for good because they feel they can contribute and it is too hard to assimilate the earthquakes in any other way. Some die unexpectedly of unusual illnesses or accidents. Some shift their investments and invest in rebuilding here, or raise money for rebuilding here.

Some of us become terrified to go in lifts, or into under ground car parks or to walk near brick walls, or to visit cities that have many tall buildings all beside each other.

Some people just pack up and leave for good. The only way for them is to start again, somewhere else. When people leave the city, the broken open feeling of the earthquakes stays inside them. They take the earthquakes with them. Sometimes they feel they can never return, even when the earthquakes have stopped for many months, even years. Most of us stay here — in our shaky turangawaewae, our place of belonging.

Kara agrees to drive with Pieter. They will take Helena to a rest home that Pieter has organised in Waimate, two and a half hours south of Christchurch. Kay was born in Waimate and she has family and friends still there who can care for Helena better than they can manage here. It is early morning as they leave. The sun is coming up in the east. They have just themselves. They have very little else left in the way of things. They have Helena in the front seat, the seat is flat back and Kara sits in the back behind Pieter, holding her hand. Pieter drives out through the back streets to Halswell and on out of the city.

Kara still has the sadness about her. Pieter tells her, "You know Kara, Saint Therese was twenty-five when she died. The same age as your son Hone. Saint Therese said, "I will spend my heaven doing good upon the earth. Maybe that is what your Hone is up to." Kara smiles as she holds Helena's hand. "I wish he was here, in his body." Pieter says, "I wouldn't wish these continuing aftershocks on anyone's body."

Pieter has very little fuel but he knows that further south there are petrol stations that are open and have not been damaged by the quake. The underground fuel tanks at the stations in the south and east of the city have been thrown up and out of the ground and are standing awry, half in half out of the ground.

As they get clear of the city and further south, they see people standing on the sides of the roads. The people have tables and tents set up. They have cakes, sandwiches, scones and cups of tea, and they offer clothes, jackets and jerseys, petrol and water to people driving out of the city. Pieter and Kara are overjoyed. They can't believe the goodness of these people.

Kara holds Helena's hand. She weeps as she sees the people standing at the sides of the road looking out for them. Pieter stops for fuel and receives a cup of tea and a hot date scone. Someone offers them another blanket for Helena. Helena can barely drink. Her face is set. She sips only a very little at a time, just barely. She is not able to eat.

All the way to Waimate there are people on the sides of the road with hot food, cold food, home baking, blankets, water, hot drinks. All the way there are people waiting, watching out for them, strangers they have never met before in their lives.

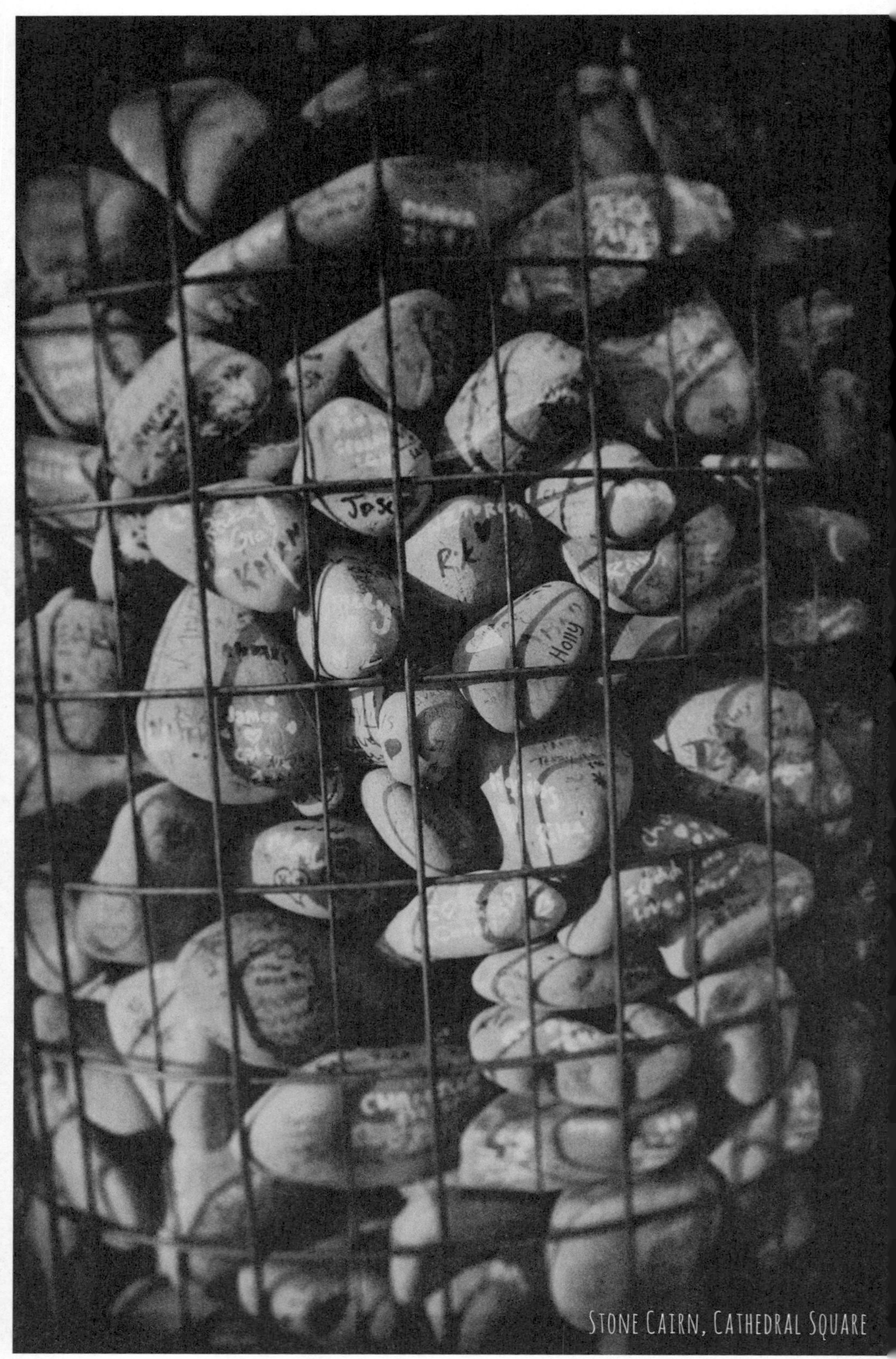

Stone Cairn, Cathedral Square

20

~Pounamu~

Greenstone Container

If we lived for a thousand years we would know about her in her many guises, but we don't, we live eighty years if we are lucky. Some folk who are from other less dynamic places don't know about this wild dancing of the earth, but we know her like this.

It is like camping. There's no electricity. Tents are the safest. Nothing can fall on you. There's no running water anywhere. Half of the pipes under the city are destroyed by the quake.

People are out walking everywhere, at dawn, at dusk, at night, during the day. People walk down by the river, or sit there, eating together, hugging strangers, holding hands, listening quietly, a deep strong love among us. It is better to be outside walking when the shaking comes, you don't hear the windows rattle, the crockery fall and break, you don't feel caught as you do inside a building.

If the earth were a sea and we were in small boats, not houses, it would all make perfect sense, this dancing, singing, the deep feelings of love and care we have for our neighbors, for random strangers. Like a bird on air you rest here on the grass, but only for a while. Never again will we take Papatuanuku, our wild Earth Mother, for granted.

The roads are cracked and closed. Often it is easier to walk. We walk by the rivers, in the gardens, under the trees, by the ocean beaches. The trees are safe, the water is cooling, calming. We walk and stop and talk, and walk, and walk. I used to wonder what the comfort in a crook and a staff was. There is comfort in the walking, in talking, in the walking with a staff in your hand. In these times, often there is nothing else, that's all the comfort there is.

Hemi sits still and quiet on the spot where he dug the girl out of the ruins, wondering how he could contact her family, let them know how it was during her last minutes. Talk with them, tell them where she was, what happened and that he did his best to get her out of the rubble and save her.

Hemi rubs absentmindedly at the earth beside him, scratches

up a bit of dirt and funnels it back down through his fingers. He does it again and again. Then he comes across something in the dust. He doesn't look down, but he traces his fingers around the shape. It is a piece of pounamu, carved, a bird, a tall slim bird. He lifts it up to the light, examines it closely and then places it in his inside pocket.

He wonders if it was hers. Hemi gets on his knees and he looks more closely at the spot where he was sitting a few minutes ago. He picks his way carefully across the patch of earth, the way he has been trained to do.

Far off across the Square there is another person in a hard hat and an orange vest. To get into the red zone, the destroyed inner city of Otautahi Christchurch, Tess has had to borrow gear from a workman. She is one of the only women in the red zone. She is walking with the help of crutches, her left ear is bandaged to her head and she has trouble feeling and directing her left leg.

Hemi sits back on his haunches. He hasn't found anything else. He pulls the long slim bird pounamu out of his inside pocket and rubs it.

Tess limps past the stone cairn. She moves her hand, touching each of the river stones as she does. She is clear that she has to come face to face with the place where she was buried. Otherwise she will never relax inside another building again.

She pours water from a bottle over her hands, and over her face.

Hemi doesn't see her. Tess makes her way over to the spot where she was buried. She doesn't want to disturb anybody or anything. Hemi feels somebody behind him. He turns and looks up. He looks again.

"Hi" says Tess.

"You are alive!" says Hemi.

Tess looks at him, curiously.

Hemi looks at her, as if he is seeing a ghost.

Tess runs her hand through her hair.

"I was here when you were under in the rubble."

"You got me out?"

"I dug you out."

"You are alive!"

"I am," says Tess. He reaches out his hand and he touches hers, it's real, alive, flesh, blood and bones.

He laughs at himself.

"You are alive!"

"Yes I am alive."

"I thought no one could survive that."

"My leg is broken, my head hurts, my insides ache."

"You are here and you are whole!"

"This is the spot?"

"Yes"

"I don't remember a lot."

Hemi feels in his inside pocket for the long slim bird piece of pounamu. He gives it to her. She looks into his eyes and smiles and cries at the same time. She holds the pounamu close to her heart. Sounds like the roll of distant thunder coming closer and closer and then the earth shakes and shakes a huge long drawn out wave of a quake. Tess screams, drops the pounamu and heads on her crutches away from the buildings and towards the cairn and the trees in the centre of the Square. Hemi leaps up, follows her and under a tree near the cairn, he stops Tess and holds her still until the shaking subsides.

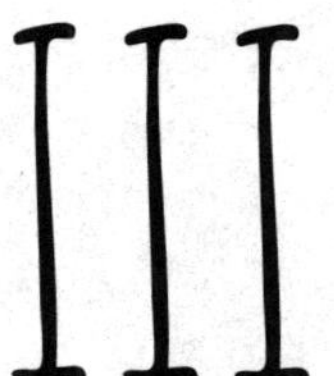

Butterflies by River

21

~Pūrerehua~

Misty
Cirrus Cloud
Moth, Butterfly
Bullroarer

You begin to see through things. Things begin to see through you. Crockery and books fly through the air, pianos spin out of control across a room, stout brick chimneys crumble, concrete fireplaces explode outwards killing, maiming and causing havoc in their wake.

We spend days taking down chimneys. Any brick chimneys left standing we dismantle. Some chimneys look okay at the top, okay from outside, but when you get up on the roof, inside the roof they are sliced clean through.

Chimneys and brick walls are dangerous, they can kill and maim people. Some of the guys get up on the roof and work fast and others stay at the bottom collecting the bricks. We pass them down from the roof one to another and stack them quickly. We want no one on the roof when another severe earthquake comes.

There are pukeko everywhere, godwits, oyster catchers, Canadian geese and odd rare birds not seen here for many years are returning not in ones or twos, but in flocks. Blue ducks whiori appear in groups on the river. Birds walk across roads in packs, not moving or flying away when a person or a car comes near. The person in the car slows, the bird continues to walk across slowly. They expect us to stop, and we do.

Pieter and Kara walk beside the river. The ducks gather in twos and threes, settling down for the night along the banks of the river. This river looks as it did before the quakes. The trees, the flowers, the flaxes are all standing right where they were. If Pieter looks along the river, and not deeply into the water and not out away from the river to where the roads and houses are, he might think all of the happenings of the last weeks are figments of his imagination.

Kara says straight away to Pieter, "Why were we spared?" Pieter replies, "Why do I live? Why does Kay die? You need to consult with God regarding these matters, Kara. God will enlighten you."

"In these circumstances, Pieter? A benevolent God active in

the world, doesn't make sense for me at this moment."

"I don't know what God is up to here. We are all brought together on our hands and knees. We can barely pick ourselves up."

"We're not at war with anybody, a good earthquake in one of the war zones might have stopped the war, but here! God is not up to anything, Pieter. This isn't what a good God would do."

"But you stay on here in this place, woken through the night by the quaking."

"I don't want to leave here, Pieter."

"Anyone can leave Kara. Everyone is replaceable sooner or later. There is a strong irresistible energy in this place that holds us here."

"I wish Hone was here, unravelling it all in bits and pieces the way he could."

"I wish Kay was here, walking, holding my hand."

They get to the spot where the butterflies gather at the time of the autumn equinox. Despite the earthquakes and all the upheaval, the butterflies have returned to the same sunny spot. The butterflies Kay found some years back, all clustered together in a warm sunny spot on the kanuka and kahikatea trees. Pieter and Kara stand and gaze at them for a long while. The butterflies gathering together, give them strength. Other folk come by, see the butterflies and stop and gaze silently too.

There is a shaking of the earth, the leaves rustle in the trees. No one has to run to any other place here, there are no buildings nearby. The river swells a little. People are still for a while, watching, waiting, they move back from the river. The butterflies wave on the leaves of the trees, back and forth with the swaying of the branches of the trees. The butterflies don't go anywhere. The quake subsides.

It's dusk. Kara and Pieter head to the fish-and-chip shop.

On the way back Kara opens the top, eats a chip, gives one to Pieter and chucks one into the air to a passing seagull. Then the seagulls are all around her. She throws up a few more chips then shuts up the packet and walks on with Pieter, away from the seagulls.

Darkness comes gently and Rehua comes out, just before they get to the turnoff. Pieter pulls out one chip. Out of nowhere there is a rustling from high in the redwood tree above the river. The seagulls have disappeared.

Pieter throws the chip very high into the air. The kahu swoops low collects Pieter's chip and then circles up and away high into the stars. Pieter smiles at the kahu. They walk on up the street with their fish and chips to what is left of their homes.

Our Lady's Grotto, Barbadoes Street

22

~Aroha~

Love

In the presence of breath

All of the young people, irrespective of background, are exceptional. They carry old people on their shoulders to safety wherever they find them, remain calm, and act with fortitude and awareness. They are still and sure.

Many small kindnesses happen everywhere with gifts of flowers and folk preparing food and dropping it off to people. Flower shops and small cafes spring up everywhere, places where someone can buy you a coffee, have a chat, calm your nerves a little, take a breath or buy you a bunch of flowers.

In these earthquakes, the entire community bands together, holds itself together, in a way that most folk in their lifetimes would never otherwise experience. We are not angry towards each other, but holding, calming, loving, and caring for each other. We care for strangers in a way that is to be celebrated and carried on forever.

Whoever comes to the door, is fed, nurtured, nourished. Gangs and tough cookies, old folk, young folk, well and unwell, all go out and help in big ways and small ways, do whatever they can. We are all in the same boat together.

Helena is lightly dozing on the bed in the Waimate Rest Home. She has clean sheets and a clean room with no cracks in it, an ordinary building that is standing, the way buildings used to. She has a new nightie and fresh blankets and they have bathed her and put her to bed. She hears feet walking lightly over the grass and across the grounds, towards her room. There is a knock at the door and she looks over. Kara is there with a bunch of white and pink daisies. Helena smiles and pulls herself up a little in bed and receives the flowers. Kara finds a vase and precious water comes pouring out of the tap. Kara places the flowers where Helena can see them. Kara boils the jug and makes Helena and herself a cup of tea.

Helena smells the scent of the white and pink daisies. Kara

talks as she makes the tea, "Most of the statues of the men have fallen down off their chairs or their horses and onto their noses. The Victoria Street clock tower is standing and the Bridge of Remembrance and the Edwardian Fountain in the Botanical Gardens with the pink flamingos."

Helena nods, listening intently to everything Kara is telling her. "Ballantynes department store will be all right, after the fire in the fifties they built it like a fortress. Nobody died in the two cathedrals either. The wonderful wooden roof of the Presbyterian Church at Carlton Mill remains standing perfectly on its wooden pillars. The brick walls have fallen. Three workmen who were repairing the organ damaged in the 4 September 2010 earthquake, died in the Methodist Church."

Kara gives Helena tea. Helena has a tiny sip. The shock has gone a little out of her face, but she is not able to eat.

"There are six grottos of Our Lady around the city. The buildings in front of the grottos are fallen down and broken. Each of the grottos is intact and Our Lady looks out onto the street from each of them. Each building in the past had hidden her from view from the street."

At this last piece of news, Helena startles and then her eyes settle and focus on Kara.

Helena brings her Rosary beads out, she motions to Kara to join her. "*Wees egroet Maria, vol van genade* Hail Mary full of grace

De Heer is met U The Lord is with you...."

Helena repeats the Hail Mary ten times, the first decade of the rosary. Kara joins in with her as best she can. Helena goes on the second, the third, the fourth, and the fifth decades. Her voice by now is threadbare and faint, but on she goes. When she is done Helena lies back in her bed, peaceful and still. She closes her eyes. Kara tucks her in, kisses her lightly on the cheek and creeps out the door.

High Street, man on roof

23

~Harihari~

TAKE, CARRY
SONG SO PEOPLE
PULL TOGETHER

Maybe Papatuanuku is simply stretching a little the way she does every hundred years or so, waking up, waking us up. We integrate this understanding of earth stretching, bit by broken bit inside of our selves. Our way of looking at the world, our response to the earth, our way of being on the earth, altered. We are being stretched, expanded, awakening.

There's no school, no university, no polytech, for three or four weeks. Everything's closed down. The earthquakes continue. All the buildings are being assessed and reassessed after each new earthquake higher than 5 on the richter scale. The roads are so broken up, it takes five or six days for most buses to start running again. Once the buses start running, hundreds of young people take spades and go to the volunteer student army spots and shovel liquefaction and mud.

There is no school for three weeks. Those schools by the rivers have severely damaged buildings. Christchurch is full of rivers. Some of the schools are totally broken and inoperable.

The entire Christchurch school system closes down. In the next three weeks, the Christchurch secondary school system and a good portion of the primary school system rearranges itself, students, books, teachers, classes, buses. The schools that have the least damage will be open in the mornings for their own students from 7.00am — 1.00pm. The damaged schools will occupy the undamaged schools in the afternoons, and their schools will run from 1.00pm — 6.00pm.

In the meantime the secondary and tertiary students and anyone else strong enough and willing enough to join them are out with shovels and spades digging through gardens, driveways, walkways and streets full of liquefaction bubbled up out of the ground.

Hemi is out at New Brighton supervising and clearing liquefaction with about twenty other young people in one old couple's garden. He has a big curving shovel. The liquefaction has turned solid and set like concrete. Each shovelful is like lifting lead, but there are hundreds of young people. They are young and strong and they work hard.

Kara drops off an extra wheelbarrow and two more shovels and takes three big quiches for their lunch. The old people of the street have hot cups of cocoa for morning tea and hot scones with raspberry jam, waiting for the young diggers. The liquefaction and mud are all over the streets and around people's houses. The student army volunteers, set up by university students, go from house to house, and street to street. A group of twenty young people go with shovels and wheelbarrows, and dig liquefaction out of people's homes, gardens, lawns and garages.

Many young people need to work together to move the set liquefaction. You can break little bits of the set liquefaction off at a time and get it into the wheelbarrows — it all adds up, so with a team of twenty you can make an impact on a whole street.

There's all sorts of young people working here with Hemi, some are covered in tattoos, some have wild hair-cuts, some have buttoned up tops and plaits, some could be fourteen years old, others twenty-eight. They all get on with it, in the sun, digging out the mud and liquefaction, that the older folk would have had no way of getting out by themselves. The liquefaction has set in and around their houses, over their driveways, right through their flower and vegetable gardens, all over the lawns.

Kara tries to dig a shovel full of liquefaction out of the garden, but it is set like concrete, she can't move an inch of it. Only the young strong folk can move it. The mud buries everything, there's nowhere to go to get away from it. By lunchtime the young folk have completed clearing the whole of the property. The older people are delighted. They thank each of the young ones. They bring out a box of chocolates and pass it around.

Hemi digs on in wonder and awe at the power of this stuff bubbling up and out of the earth and then setting like stone. He wonders if it's any good for his garden. And then he sees her. He is certain it is her. The way she holds her head, slightly to the side, just very slightly.

She is dishing out vege soup to the student army. She's sitting down and she has a crutch by her side, but she's here. He gets in her queue, lines up with everyone else, and when he gets to her, he holds out his plate. She recognises him this time and gives him his soup and smiles. Hemi slips her, on a piece of paper, under the plate, his phone number.

Then he walks off back to his soup and shoveling and wonders if she will contact him. He can't stop thinking about her all afternoon. She has the most beautiful brown eyes, and when she smiles, Hemi catches himself and laughs at himself. To distract himself, Hemi makes up a song. He gets the chorus going with his work crew and they sing new verses as they come to mind

"Chorus : Out of the rubble you come
and you know you're alive

Pipes broken pipes twisted
Pipes thrown side to side
Half the sewerage is shot
In the whole of the city

Young folk carry old people down stairs
Out of the broken houses
Down fire escapes out of the hospitals
Some still in their beds

No electricity no running water
We light fires outside we drink tea
We hold hands we hug together
We tell stories

By torchlight and candles
In ambulances and aeroplanes
We move the sick people out of the city
At dawn at dusk at 4am

No sewerage, dig a hole
In the ground
Cover the shit with leaves and soil
Build a wall build a roof, hang a door

Liquefaction sets like stone, young men,
Young women, thousands of them come
With picks shovels and axes dig the dried out silt
Burying gardens houses and cars

Again and again the liquefaction bubbles up
Again thousands of young people come
With their strength and their song
Folk bring them tea and tucker

All the chimneys fail, some tip
Some stand half upright
Bricks falling through houses trap people
Injure folk chimneys kill people

We move from house to house
Dismantling chimneys all chimneys any chimneys
One chimney looks fine outside
Underneath it is sliced simply in two

A crack opens wide
The house splits in half
The grandfather clock
Sinks into the hole

The car tips and flips into the hole
Two women climb ashen faced
Out of the windows
Of the car in the hole

A small girl is lost she is held and passed
From one to another, fed, sung to,
Until her Mother finds her with a stranger
Kisses her daughter and the stranger

The river rises up, floods its banks, then turns
And flows down the street as it quakes
People rush out of their houses into the street
Then run inside away from the raging river

At five o'clock, the young people are done for the day. They pack up their gear, and return to base. She's not there. Hemi wonders if he will see her again.

Cliff Flowers, Mount Pleasant

24

~Taonga~

Treasure

Goods, possessions

Something prized

The earthquakes are seductive. They pull you in, earth shattering, seismic, awesome, intense. They turn you over and over, around about, upside down, and spill you out. Utterly consumed, totally exposed as if you have been five hundred days in the desert sun and been sipping water and eating herbs, and you come back unrecognisable. It is a disturbing, magical, mysterious, destructive, haunting, beautiful, riveting, unable to turn your gaze away from process.

It's difficult to be away from them for a long time. You wonder what is going on in Christchurch. Which old buildings are coming down, which new buildings are going up. Which streets are repaired, and which cafes or shops are opening and where. Everything is fluid. Things change radically within days. Which part of the city did the last earthquake hit? Is a new earthquake sequence beginning, or are these aftershocks from the previous sequence?

Buildings fall down but the trees remain standing. Buildings surrounded by trees do well. The Museum buildings are set among hundred year old trees. Ninety-five percent of the taonga, the treasures in the Museum surrounded by a botanic garden of trees, are intact.

In South Canterbury one hundred kilometres south of the epicentres, most of the old buildings are standing. It feels strange to Pieter. Helena is lying in the early morning sunshine on the bed. She is well wrapped up. Pieter is humming to himself, an old tune from his youth on the shores of a beach in Holland. He can see it all in his mind's eye, as it was when he was a boy. All his people there have died now.

He has no wish to return to Holland. He is happy in New Zealand. He gives Helena small sips from the cup, but she can barely open her mouth and he thinks she is maybe not swallowing at all.

Pieter sits with Helena. He brushes her hair. She has her eyes open but he feels she is not here with him at all. She was peaceful when he came in last night with the fish and chips. She didn't want to eat even one chip. She has not been swallowing these last few days.

Pieter barely sips his tea. He reads the crossword to himself. He can't think of one solution, so he puts it down. He picks up the rest of the paper. He can't concentrate to read even a line or two, only the headlines. Spectacular, earth shattering headlines, and he is unmoved.

Pieter sits silently drinking his tea. He puts his cup down and takes Helena's hand carefully in his own. Her breathing is shallow and difficult now. They called it the death rattle, this sound. He remembers it from many years ago on a different island in another hemisphere, as a young man, with his father.

He holds Helena's hand and prays with her. He feels Mary, Our Lady all around. He asks Our Lady to bless Helena as she passes through. Helena's breathing becomes shallower and shallower and then her breathing stops.

Pieter holds her hand in his and he prays for her. Pieter closes Helena's eyes and places her hands together. He settles her blankets and her hair. He kisses her forehead. Helena's face has a radiance. All about her is a dappled light.

Arts Centre

25

~Kowhai~

Kowhai blossom

flower, tree

yellow

There are kowhai plantings on the tracks up into the Cashmere hills and across the other side of the Plains into the Southern Alps. Folk use kowhai trees blooming, as markers to ensure it is safe to travel there in the spring, after the snow has gone and the risk of avalanche has passed. Kowhai trees in flower show you when it is safe to move on to the next place in the mountains.

It snows lightly, softly. It is August. Some kowhai in sheltered places have early blossom. It is now the great snow comes and we are buried a good four days under snow. You can't see the destruction of the city. The city is quiet and still and beautiful, covered in snow.

It is early spring. Some kowhai trees are in bloom. The blossoms are brilliant golden yellow. The kowhai blooms in the area as it becomes free of frost and snow.

They ask Hemi, "Do you know now, when they will stop?"
Hemi replies, "An eighteen month period of earthquakes hit Christchurch in 1869 and all through 1870. This could be a repetition of that sequence, maybe."

"You're a geologist, you study these things, you should know with some certainty."

"That quake was a strike-slip event with oblique motion — mostly horizontal movement with some vertical movement, with reverse thrust. This has been an unusual series of earthquake sequences."

"You don't know what to expect next?"

"We have been studying the three major faults. There is a gap."

"A gap. What does that mean?"

"A gap that's all, just a gap."

"I understand you are considering leaving the city, taking extended leave."

"I have study to do overseas."

"You believe there will be more earthquakes so you are going away while they continue."

"I need to examine other locations with similar earthquake sequences."

"We have experienced 7000 earthquakes so far, how many more do you think?"

"They could go on for years, or for another three months."

"You have no idea at all?"

"There is a one in ten chance they could go on for thirty years."

"You have described what is happening, what has happened. Any indication or thought as to what will happen next?"

"It is highly probable that there will be more earthquakes."

"More large ones to come?"

"Yes."

"You're heading off for a break from the quakes? Going off to do some research some place else? Surely we are the earthquake laboratory right here. Are you finding the sheer number of earthquakes a bit much? You didn't expect new fault lines to open up? It's not quieting down the way you guys predicted at first."

"One fault line settles down and then some place else around the city another one opens up."

"And then there is the gap? "

"Normally you get a real big earthquake and the following aftershocks are all smaller and the earth settles back down again. It hasn't been like that here. One sequence of a major earthquake and its aftershocks ends, and then another major fault opens up in a totally different place around the city, with its own aftershock sequence. The gap is a problem. Another major fault may appear there. There are several possibilities."

"Do you think the whole city should be evacuated?"

"How would we do that?"

"But we understand you want to take leave."

"I do."

Rock veil, Redcliffs

26

~Ngaio~ Blossom Tree

Look carefully at

All through winter, the ngaio tree leaves remain yellow green. Their sap sinks deep into the not so quiet earth we now inhabit. Ngaio trees stand in rocks along the beaches, in rocky ledges and high on the hills and cliffs. Ngaio trees grow in the most dry and inhospitable of places with no or very little water. They look as though they have stood there forever. Nga Io, is the nothingness from which everything springs. On some cliff faces, there is nothing left but ngaio trees.

At Redcliffs, huge rocks crumble down onto the back of the primary school, taking houses with them. Cliffs split and break open above Sumner village and on Clifton Hill. Rocks from the cliffs rumble and crumble across the roads and on to the beaches from above the Sumner Surf Club. Green leaved ngaio trees remain standing among the rocks. Some are bent and twisted, some in the more sheltered places are tall and long limbed, others short and bushy.

With a little help from Hemi and a couple of his mates, Pieter has made a casket for Helena. They have painted the casket blue, Our Lady's blue. Hemi drives with the casket down to Waimate and picks up Pieter. They bring Helena back to Christchurch to Pieter's house.

Kara comes by with some kai, six candles and a bunch of flowers. She picks up Pieter's newspaper at the gate. She knocks, pops her head in the door. Pieter is lying on the couch. He is sound asleep. "Heh, Pieter."

Pieter yawns and rubs his eyes,

"Good morning, Kara."

Kara places the flowers gently on the table by Helena, "Nga mihi aroha, Pieter." Pieter sits up and rubs his head.

"She went peacefully." He can't say anymore. Pieter just sits quietly there, on the side of the couch. He's worn to the bone. Kara puts on the jug and makes Pieter a cup of tea. She pulls out the newspaper from her bag, and places it near Pieter.

Helena is lying on the deck outside the door. Kara places the flowers and the six candles around the casket. Pieter can't even manage a smile. He sips his tea. He rubs his face with his hands, straightens his hair, pulls down his shirt, "Good morning, Kara."

"Ata marie, Pieter."

Kara leaves a pot of stew, spuds, kumara, carrots, silver beet and a bit of lamb, on the stove for Pieter to heat and eat when he is able. She kisses him on the cheek and takes her leave. He says barely, "Thank you Kara."

She leaves her poem with Pieter.

Everything no matter how
it appears at the time
Everything is in God and of God
Every utterable and unutterable thing
moves towards goodness
is inside of Godness

This holy mountain
this blessed blade of grass
Everything here is holy
Hone's passing, Kay's passing
Helena's passing
These huge earth quakings

COLUMNS CURVING, MONKS SPUR

27

~MANA~

POWER

PSYCHIC FORCE

The glass in our windows is not solid but liquid. I see the glass turn into fluid when I am standing in my aunty's house at the epicentre of a 6.2 earthquake. It is a 5 kilometre shallow earthquake, centred right below us. We are in my aunty's dining room, right on the epicentre. The glass in the windows doesn't shatter. It becomes fluid as water sparkling in the sun, molten sparkling water flowing inside the window frame. If glass becomes liquid what happens to us, to our bodies, to our minds, when we vibrate at the epicentre of an earthquake?

The table and everything on it roar away from us across the room. We grab and hold each other tight, frog walking across the dancing, rolling, swaying room that is compressing like a sandwich with each jerky move we make. The roof and the floor come closer and closer together. We run down the steps and away from the building, the lampposts and to bare ground. We sit huddled together watching the dust and smoke rise up over the city, the lampposts dancing oddly, the wires swinging, cracks opening in the road beneath us. It feels like a hundred years pass before the earthquake stops, but in watch time it is only minutes or seconds. I am too terrified to return to the house for weeks. She is so brave, my eighty-two year old aunty, she goes back in and sleeps there that night.

When I do return to her house the glass has reverted to a seemingly solid consistency. It is no longer fluid. The dancing, breathing, sandwiching woodwork has not broken, the house stands in one piece, with some odd cracks here and there.

I am certain now that nothing is fixed and rigid, all is still and moving. The wood here flexes, breathes in and out. Our houses can dance and they can be still. Wood and glass are fluid, breathing, living things, just depends when your gaze lights upon them. It depends when they are vibrating or at what frequency. They can be solid, fluid. They can hold together or they can spring apart.

Kara is walking on Sumner beach by Rapanui, when another quake comes. Bits of cliffs come down and dust rises into the air. Out of her mouth comes a great weeping cry. She calls out as if from Papatuanuku, our mother, the earth, herself. Hemi comes looking for Kara. He knows Kara will be at the beach. The epicenter is not far from where she will be. Everywhere there are roads down and roadblocks going up.

Along Ferry Road the earth opens up, cars sink into the road where they were parked, in slow motion they sink, people crawl out the car windows and onto the roofs, on and on the cars sink. The water and mud feel as if the sea is coming in and in from the river and the estuary, until it is everywhere, as if it belonged there. Hemi turns and decides to drive through the Heathcote Valley. As he drives, he comes across boulders bounced onto the road. He drives around the boulders. The rest of the world is driving the other way, away from the beach, away from a possible tsunami. Hemi drives on.

He knows where Kara will be. She has taken him here many times, all through his life from when he was a small boy. He wonders how high the ocean is, or if the waves are crashing, or if it is flat, sucking in and out. He knows she will be calling there. He knows this is the place of her calling, the way it comes through her, not of her own making. He knows the voices, hears the sounds. This time Hemi knows he needs to be at her side.

He knows Hone will be there, in whatever shape he has taken. Hemi drives on around the boulders and shards of glass and houses. The bridge is open, a couple of huge cranes are swaying drunkenly above it, but it is still open. Above Redcliffs School, the cliff has fallen, more cracks open, more houses slipping and falling down the cliffs. At least the school has been evacuated with the previous earthquakes.

Hemi inches carefully along, watching out for rock fall. He parks by the yacht club and walks from there toward Sumner beach. There is a lone figure standing by Rapanui. Bare feet, long black hair waving in the breeze, she is standing still, listening to the rock. The tide has gone out, sucked out its breath.

He wonders how long does it suck out for before it pours back in like thunder, but it's out and he prays it will stay out. Rapanui doesn't reveal the old waka shape, the form of an ure, it held before the quakes. It is a broken prow, it has shed its skin, the shape curving upwards, a tongue pokes upwards out of the rocky bed. He sees another rocky shape near Rapanui, almost that of a small flower.

"Whaea!"

"Haere mai, nau mai, Hemi, e pai ana koe?"

"What are you doing here, e Whaea, everyone else is fleeing!"

"*Ko tenei te wa o te hurihuri o te ao*. This is the place of the turning of the world." Kara turns then to Rapakai and and the karanga floods from her, "*Whakarongo whakarongo* Listen listen
Whakarongo mai ra Listen to me
Koutou nga taurekareka you rascals
E takahi nei who trample
I te mana tangata the mana of the people
Mana whenua the mana of the earth
Mana taiao e the mana of nature
Kati ra te kohuru enough of the treacherous killing
I nga mokopuna of our grandchildren
Tukino i nga moutere destruction of our islands
Te Moana-Nui-a-Kiwa our Pacific Ocean
Aue Aue Aue Hi."

Seagulls, Estuary

28

~AWA~

River

Incantation to still a storm

I have a dream. I am gathering flax for papermaking and working just up above the riverbank. The tools and large frame are all on the bank by the river. There is another woman far out across the river, in the water. She is doing work also, to do with the making of paper.

I look down and see the river flooding its banks, collecting all of our tools in its path. I head towards the river and suddenly it turns and flows in the opposite direction taking all of our papermaking tools with it.

Myself and the other woman run after the gear. A tall young man, all in white and shining appears from behind a tree. I know he is my son. He jumps into the swollen river and retrieves all of our gear. We go down and help bring it all up onto the higher ground.

All of the gear is safe. The river is flowing swiftly, full of uprooted trees. When he is sure we are all are safe and our work materials are accessible, the young man disappears into the sky. We begin our work again, but the river continues flowing swiftly in the opposite direction. It never returns to flow the old way.

Hemi stands alongside of Kara. He gazes far out to sea. They walk up and sit on the high rock by the track.

Hemi says, "We are like ants crawling on the surface."

"We are worse and better than ants Hemi. We cause more trouble than ants crawling on the surface of Papatuanuku. We receive the breath when we come in. We have imagination. We can see forwards and backwards in time. We can imagine across time. We can see other places, other worlds. We can hear stories and they come to life inside of us."

"We are nothing to her, Whaea. She doesn't care if we live or we die. We are not part of her grand plan. Papatuanuku will go on and on irrespective of us living or dying."

"We are everything and nothing to her. We are part of her being, of her way forward and we have some choice in how we respond."

"You die, Whaea, then you evolve. Or you evolve, then you die."

"If I flow with her, Hemi, it is like stepping into a river. A river of earth, mud, wood, shards of broken glass, metal, bouncing boulders and waves. In a river you sink or you swim. You might try and hold fast to a rock or a tree branch, but the river flows on, twisting and turning. It doesn't stop for you. Your arms get tired and worn out trying to hold on, or the branch breaks and you get swept away by the river. But is it such a bad thing to be swept away and along by the river? You can scream and wave your arms and legs about, use up your breath, hoping someone will jump in and drag you out of the river or you can lie on your back or float on your tummy and let the river carry you."

"This is a fast moving, raging river that we are in, Whaea. Don't you reckon we could jump out, catch our breath, rest a while, and get our feet on some solid earth, just to feel ordinary? There's a conference on disasters in Singapore. I could go and you could come with me. We could stay on there until this raging river slows down."

Kara smiles, "Thank you for thinking of me, Hemi."

"We could stay away for a good few months, or a year or two maybe, until the earthquakes are all over."

"Do you think if you take me a long long way away they might stop? Do you think I am a cause of the trouble here?"

"No, Whaea. We are burnt-out and these quakes are not going to stop anytime soon. The epicentre of the quakes has circled around and through the centre of the city. It is causing huge destruction to central, south and east Christchurch, the port, the beaches and the rivers. It is a good idea to clear off for a while."

"Thank you, Hemi, but I will be here. There is no other place I have to be. This is my place."

"You know, Whaea, that the quakes could get worse. They are hitting this area here along the beaches now. The chance of a tsunami right here is very high." Kara says nothing.

Hemi goes on, "That's why I came out here. To pick you up."

"I am happy here, Hemi."

"I am not happy for you to be here, Whaea, come back with me to Redcliffs. You have done what you came here to do."

"I am staying here."

"You could get swept away by the ocean. There is a tsunami warning out. Didn't you hear the sirens before?"

"No I didn't."

"You need to come with me this time, Whaea."

"I'm staying here."

"There's work that needs to be done, change to be made, and you want to be alive."

"I'm finished Hemi. I don't want to change anything, do anything, fix anything. I want to just stay here. I don't care if the sea comes in."

"Hone wants you to leave, to come with me now."

"Hone? Where is he?"

Hemi motions Kara to look toward the Redcliff Yacht club and there is Hone, or someone the spitting image of him walking along the track above the rocks.

"I will come Hemi."

Kara goes down and washes her face and hands with water, she blesses the rock, the earth, the sea and the sky and she turns and walks off along the track with Hemi. They arrive at the Redcliff Yacht Club. Hone is no longer there. He is gone. He, or the person just like him, has disappeared.

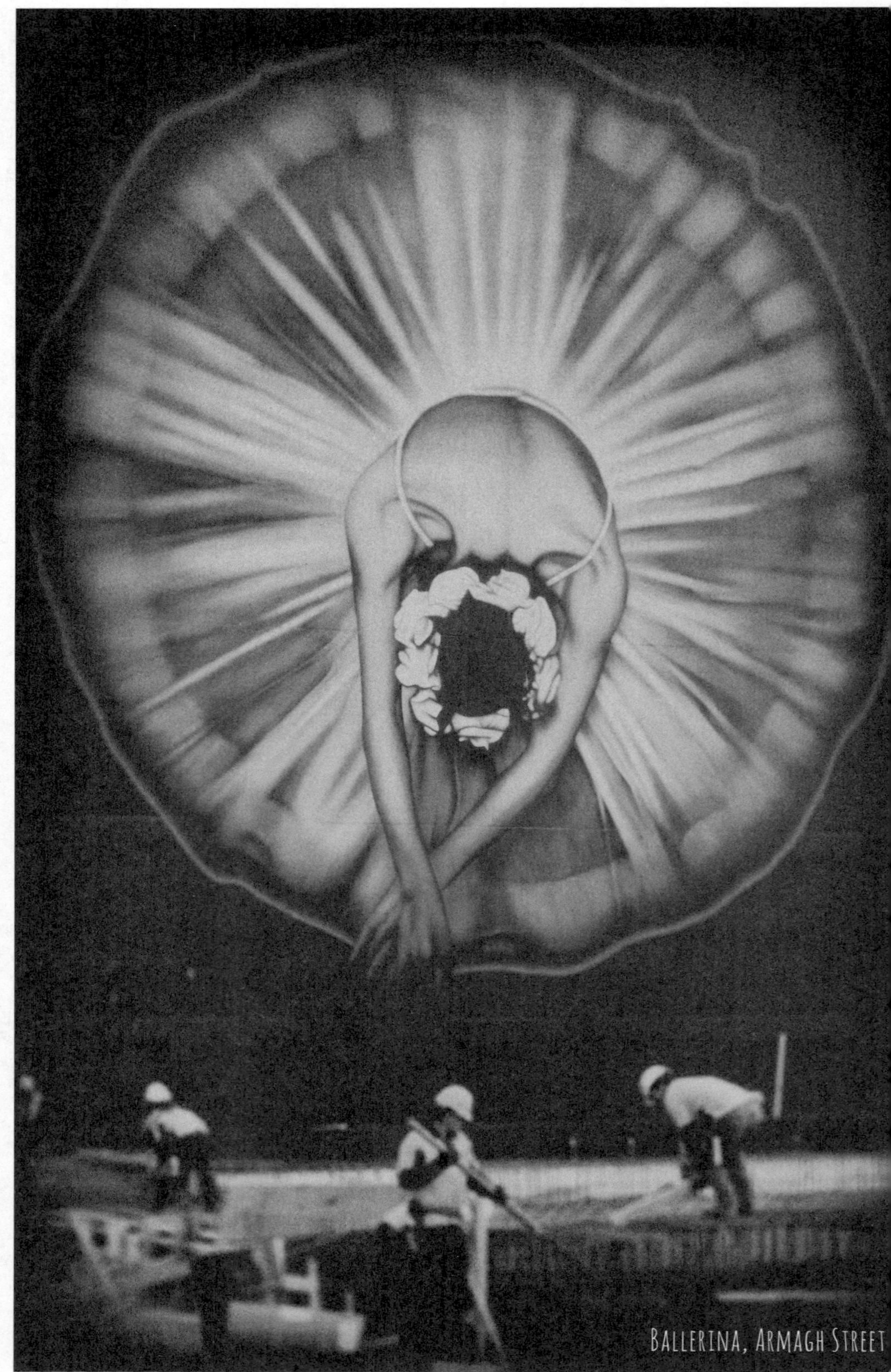

Ballerina, Armagh Street

29

~Ataahua~
Beautiful Shape of the Dawn

Is this how God does it, rips us apart, takes everything away so we are fresh and new and open. Is this how God is revealed to us? Shedding everything I loved, I once held dear, everything I once delighted in.

We come from the sea and the air we go back to the sea and to the air, when our time here walking on the earth, in these bodies, is done. I know you come by often, in a rainbow, as a kotuku or sometimes as a blue heron. Sometimes when I am sitting still and quiet in the night, you play a note on your old guitar, or flick the lights on and off, just to let me know you are around and I am not alone.

Here, located as we are on the Pacific Ring of Fire, people develop a sixth sense, a knowing, about the way the earth truly is, because we do not experience her as still and stable. All manner of things are flowing through her, and through us.

I am feeling my way back inside my body. It has taken me a long while to find my way back. All of these odd pains racking my body, ear aching, back aching, hip twinging, knee twisting, sinusitis, tooth aches, riddling my body in different places, trying to pull me back into touching and awareness of my body.

Neuroscientist Michael Morzenish says the conscious mind weaves patterns of thought, and our subconscious receives and holds these patterns as vibrational imprints. Our whole city, of 400,000 people, has been receiving continuous repetitive vibrational imprints from the earthquake sequences for twenty months.

I feel fear in every pore, every ravaged aching part — ankles, hip, back, neck, static in my head. My body is too sore, too full of pain in unknowable places. This time I have to be still and listen. I need to be quiet and true to this sacred time, this darkness, this still warm dark rain, this Mother Whaea time, this deep spring.

My body won't let me enter into a blind sea of activity. I need to stay with spring pinpricking the deep dark blue night sky, stars lighting the way, tulips appearing, pure white cherry blossoms, rain falling softly.

Tess is sitting on the rock wall at Redcliffs looking out over the estuary. She's sitting there with her crutches by her side, gazing at the sea, the sky, the great white snow mountains, as if nothing at all was bothering her. What else do you do on a fine sunny day?

Tess is happy that today, despite all the big quaking and shaking going on, she is not lying beneath a pile of rubble with the dim certainty that nobody is ever going to pull her out. She can see the water and the sky. She can't hear any voices and that is just fine. She is not desperate to hear voices, as she was then. She smiles to herself and rubs her hand through her hair.

Tess turns slightly and sees Hemi walking with someone in her direction. She sees Hemi and he smiles at her. She smiles back. He goes over to her and kisses her lightly on the cheek. Tess glows.

"This is my friend Tess, Whaea." He introduces Tess to Kara. Kara gives Tess a warm hug. They sit on the rock wall by Tess. All the cars are streaming towards the city alongside them. Hemi asks, "You're not heading anywhere Tess?'

"I feel safe here."

"Hemi doesn't think it's safe here," Kara says.

Hemi says, "I think we should all go away for a while, take a good break."

"You don't think they will settle down anytime soon?" asks Tess.

"If I go on study leave, I might find out more about what is going on with the earth here."

"I think if I stay close here, I might get to hear her," Kara says.

"Thank you for pulling me out of the rubble, Hemi. Some people are leaving, they can't stand the shaking anymore, but I think it will go with you wherever you go. I just come down here and chill out by the sea. That's what I do."

"You are very brave, Tess," Kara says.

"Me he kōrinorino kōkopu Tess," says Hemi.

Kara smiles. Tess looks curiously at Hemi.

"You are like a beautiful mottled trout Tess. You shimmer delicately as you move."

"I am a beautiful mottled trout?" says Tess hesitantly.

"You are beautiful Tess," says Hemi. Tess doesn't know what to say. She smiles at Hemi. "I don't feel very brave, or beautiful."

"You are beautiful," says Hemi. And when he says it, Tess feels beautiful.

Kara leaves them there together, by the rock wall.

IV

Face in wall, Square

30

~Ahi Kā~

Fires Burning Occupying

I am a tiny caterpillar wandering around on a sleeping, living, breathing giantess. Doing my daily tasks as if they were important, as if they had meaning. While the giantess sleeps and has pleasant dreams and doesn't move much in her sleep, staying peacefully on her right side, I am all right, I live and dream and work and things go more or less smoothly.

But if something disturbs her sleep, a bird calling early in the morn wakens her, or she has a strange dream, and she moves fitfully, or decides to do a haka, it's difficult for me. Being a tiny insect trying to do the dishes, wash the clothes, feed the children, get to work, plant the potatoes, on the body of a fitfully moving giantess, gets difficult.

On 22 February 2011, one hundred and eighty-nine die, and more than two thousand people are injured, some loosing limbs and mobility. In the days and weeks and months and years that follow the eighteen months of severe earthquakes, hundreds more of us die prematurely, thousands more become ill. We suffer premature heart attacks, odd cancers, unusual accidents, broken heartedness, recurring depressions, life destroying strokes, job loss, loss of home, mental break downs, loss of meaning, insomnia, teeth falling out, strange itches, and aching pains. We manifest strange collections of illnesses, we become emotionally, physically, mentally, spiritually disturbed, highly sensitised, altered.

Some folk have only a small crack above and on either side of a door, in the middle of the house that takes all the stress and strain of the shaking. Other people have deep wide house-broken-open-in-half cracks or house-broken-in-four cracks as if lightning has danced patterns through their house. Some of us have cracks on our surface, maybe a cut or a break. But underneath the surface, we don't know what severe structural damage is concealed. As time progresses we begin to see clearly all the damage, to ourselves and to our buildings, underneath. It slowly but surely swings into focus, the light reveals the underneath and we see.

On a world scale we are tiny. We don't have millions of people in our city. We don't have hundreds of thousands dead and tens of thousands injured. We have an Earthquake Commission. With all its imperfections, we have one. 99 percent of us were insured. Very few countries even have insurance for those who live in earthquake affected regions.

From the view of the giantess, I am tiny. As a small caterpillar, living on her ocean of a body, I can see, I can observe and discern stars, lights and pathways in the sky. I can watch her, feel her move, and try to make sense of her movements, her erratic shakings.

Tess and Hemi are left sitting on the rock wall above the water.

"Good to see you, Hemi."

"Thank you, Tess. You just appear out of the blue, like you drop out of the sky, right in front of me."

"I come out here, because I need to be somewhere I can see sea and sky and have no buildings anywhere near me. How come you just turn up, the next big earthquake, here you are, right beside me again! This time I'm not buried and you don't have to dig me out."

"I can't believe you are alive and sitting here alive beside me." He takes her hand in his two hands and kisses her hand. Tess smiles.

"I was thinking Tess of heading off to do some research,"

"Oh"

"Why do you say oh?"

"I like you turning up in odd places around the city. I like being around you."

"We could have a long distance relationship."

"I don't do distance, not now. Things have changed inside me since being in that hole under the rubble."

"E-mails, skype, phone calls, visiting."

"Yeah but it's not the daily bread. It's just the highlights. If I'm going to go with someone now, I need them here, right beside me."

Hemi takes Tess's hand in his.

"It's my work,"

"I know. Best not to start anything. If you're going away."

"You don't do long distance relationships?"

"Not now."

"Okay. But if I was to be living here maybe you would like to go out with me?"

"I would like to go out with you."

Hemi squeezes her hand lightly. Tess pecks him gently on the nose. "Well then."

"I guess I better wander off Hemi. The rubble might be out looking for me."

"I can take you."

"Better not. Have a good safe journey to wherever it is you are going."

She squeezes his hand and they hongi. Hemi kisses Tess on the cheek and she leaves.

Hemi sits there by himself on the rock wall. He sees the sun shining on the white snowy mountains across the water. He sees the white caps of the surf breaking at the spit. He likes the warm feeling in his heart. Hemi watches a yacht nodding on the tide as the tide comes in and he nods with the yacht and he remembers Tess's cheek on his lips and his heart feels good inside.

Blue Bird, Chalice, Cathedral Square

31

~HUA~

FRUIT
EGG OF BIRD
ROE OF FISH

Deep, deep, deeper still, not one leaf left on the branches of the cherry tree, but a tiny dark red crimson bud hinting spring, fruiting in the depth of winter. Naked the cherry tree, open to the sky, but for this tiny bud. The walnut tree is barely clothed in ragged leaves, brown and speckled yellow brown bark, some old walnuts hanging still in their dark decaying sheaths, spindly leaves dancing lightly in the breeze as if to tease. Deep winter solstice is seven days gone.

Inside by the roaring fire of wood burning, I remove my gloves and hat, coat and boots. I come before the fire of tree branches burning, and bare myself. I am learning to describe the edges of the hole your passing makes in me. At first, I was engulfed. I could see no edge. Now I can begin to describe the edges of the hole. They are tangled and smudged where the tears have rained like snow. But they are melting and I can begin to make them out, ragged and almost whole.

Pieter is wandering around alone and in circles and is not sure how to proceed. He is uncertain what to do anymore. Many of his customers have disappeared into thin air. They have left the city, with no work, no school, nothing on, and taken their kids and themselves away from the shakes.

There are deep cracks and curves and holes in the streets outside Pieter's shop. The earth can open wide at any moment and take anything or anyone it wants. This morning Pieter walks down to the river and back three times. He goes to the spot where the monarch butterflies gather. Every year they gather here together irrespective of earthquakes, droughts, or torrential downpours. They know how to go on, but Pieter is not sure how to go on, in this very different world.

Pieter sits down with his little burner and boils himself hot water for a cup of tea. It is a sunny, spring morning. All the birds are singing. The daffodils are coming out along the river, the kowhai exquisite, the blossom blooming white, the early pink blossom is just coming on the trees. The birds and insects are in a state of pure delight.

Pieter wonders what on earth to do in this new sort of a life. He doesn't feel up to a new beginning. He feels like a baby coming in with nothing but the flesh he stands up in. He has to make his way all over again. Maybe, he thinks, I have gained a bit of wisdom. I have been around here for a while. I have seen a few things in my time. I know how to move my hands, my legs. How to grasp objects, how to walk, how to talk. I don't have to relearn everything over again.

Pieter thinks, but I have nothing, no one left. Everything is broken. The shaking goes on and on. I am here. I don't want to be anywhere else. He sits outside in the sun, sips his tea and reads the newspaper. Kara walks along the road, and comes to the spot where Pieter's shop once stood.

"Where can I get the milk and newspaper, Pieter?" Pieter gives Kara his newspaper.

"They're all gone," says Pieter, "Strange isn't it how I come into the world, and there's all these folk around me. Now they are all gone and I am left here."

A korimako bellbird comes and settles in the tree above Pieter's head. He doesn't notice her. Kara sees the korimako. The korimako sings a song to Pieter. Kara listens. Pieter stops talking, Pieter follows Kara's line of vision and sees the korimako singing directly above his head. The korimako finishes her song and leaves, Pieter smiles barely, but he smiles.

"You know, Kara, I came here forty years ago. The moment I put my foot on the ground here, I knew I would never leave." Pieter pours Kara a cup of tea.

Kara sips and talks, "Christchurch, Otautahi is the place folk come to, when they need a change of heart, of direction, a shift in their way of seeing things, a new opening. This is a place where new ideas well up and come through into the world."

"But I am just trying to live out my life here. It's nothing special," says Pieter, "It's like any other place. You get up have your breakfast, read the paper, go to work."

"Sometimes new ideas are blocked for a while, but then the opening is unblocked and they pour through again. This place is a birthing canal."

Pieter says thoughtfully, "There are other places in the world where new ideas come through."

Kara talks on, "This is one of those places. Some people are drawn here. It's hard to live an ordinary life in these sacred places. The sacredness of place disrupts the ordinary."

Small pieces of understanding drift across the blue, blue sky, like tiny floating clouds of clarity. Pieter is quiet for a long time. Eventually Pieter speaks, "Nothing feels ordinary to me anymore. Everything is gone, disrupted, in confusion. People have died and disappeared. Things, buildings, houses, cars are broken or disappeared or fallen over. Sometimes I don't even know which street I'm on. In many places there is not one recognisable landmark left. The lampposts are askew. The roads are broken. Things don't matter much anymore, only people."

"You have half a house, Pieter."

"I have half a house. I live as if it is an ordinary thing to have half a house."

"Very ordinary."

"Is this not a mysterious practice Kara, to live as if it is an ordinary thing to have half a house?"

Pieter laughs. Kara laughs.

"It is a very mysterious practice, Pieter," Kara says, "to try and live here at all."

Urban farm, High Street

32

~Wā~

Place Time

We have a strange feeling about us, as if we have all been asleep together in some odd collective dreamtime, sleeping, while our unknown insides have come out and revealed themselves whole and to the world. Each and every one of us is slowly imperceptibly waking up, shaken, almost but not quite whole, awakening.

All the things you do in the time of the earthquake, you couldn't normally have done in ordinary time. Getting to safe places, getting people out, turning electricity off, grabbing torch, water, food, checking everyone is safe, are all done in a brief few forty-six "seconds" of linear time.

Newton says waking time and space can appear linear to our senses. Albert Einstein writes "People like us who believe in physics, know that the distinction between past, present, and future is only a stubborn persistent illusion." In quantum reality, time past, present and future exist simultaneously and are interchangeable.

When I was younger, I stayed on the big marae at Ngaruawahia for a whole week. I didn't leave the marae during all of that time. When I came home I felt as if I had been away for months. I was unable to shake the feeling. Time inside the marae moved more slowly, than time outside the marae.

When I go to hit a fly on my arm, the fly experiences me as moving my hand in slow motion, so it is easy for the fly to fly away. I am a living being, moving alongside and in a different time frame. The fly is alert to differences in my breathing, the sounds I make before I begin to move. Although our experiences are simultaneous, the fly experiences the action more intimately. The fly is alert to my fast movement as if it is an extremely slow movement.

Mountains are moving living beings. They grow and live their natural life cycles, just as we do. Except that we grow inside another time frame, simultaneously, side by side, alongside the mountain. As our life cycle is to a bird's life cycle, so is a mountain's life cycle to ours.

For us time passes more slowly than for a mountain. For a bird, time passes more slowly than for us. John Kehoe says that in quantum reality, time and space are not separate from each other. Time and space exist simultaneously in one continuum. In Maori, the word for time and for space is the same word, te wa.

Einstein says time is not constant. Time changes in different reference frames, different circumstances. Sequences of moments happen, but not necessarily in linear order, at regular intervals. When objects travel at faster speeds, time slows down. When the earthquakes are happening, we are vibrating at high speed. Time slows down.

Hemi is walking along the river inside the red zone. He is wearing the orange high viz vest and yellow hard hat and boots. The interviewer and camera crew are alongside him.

Hemi, "We don't need to be running on this dirty stuff anymore. The whole of Palmerston North could be run on the wind farm beside it, all the vehicles, the factories, the commercial buildings, the houses. We could run Christchurch totally on electricity. There is a surplus of electricity produced in the South Island. We could run everything, all the buildings, all the machines, all communications, on clean energy. No fossil fuels, no oil, no gas, no coal."

"What are you on about, Hemi?"

Hemi argues on, "We get a time frame worked out, a think tank up and running and then it's done. We have a blank slate here, a fresh start, a clean start. We can make this city a clean city. We've been given a precious opportunity."

"But!"

"But what?"

"But it's never been done before."

"Germany runs half of their summer power from solar energy. Our weather conditions are much better for solar power than German weather conditions and we have fewer people."

"But it has not been done here before."

"Let's focus on Christchurch. Most of the underground infrastructure has to be rebuilt. Our rebuilt petrol stations can become electric car charging stations. We install light electric rail on the existing railways, and cycle ways alongside all the railway lines."

"People have nowhere to live. The infrastructure of the city is destroyed. Most of the CBD is down, and you talk about electric cars!"

Hemi, "People will come from all over the world to find out how we've done it. They will want to experience first hand the first oil, gas and coal free city in the world."

"There's no way we can do it."

"We've just done 30,000 earthquakes. I'm sure there's plenty of ways we could do it."

"We have to look after people first. You are distracting us from the task at hand."

"What is wrong with you Hemi?"

"Are you receiving gifts from the large coal, oil, and gas companies? You know what I mean, nice dinners, trips to exotic places, tickets for major concerts in their boxes, big sporting events. Have you become friends with the lobbyists, the major players, the major stakeholders, so you don't like to upset them, put them in the applecart. What has happened to your dreams, your vision, your integrity?"

"How does this solve our immediate problems?"

"We come up with innovative, environmentally friendly solutions. I am not proposing you'd live in a tree. You would live in a house. Your house would be smaller, sunnier and warmer. The waterways would be unpolluted, and the vehicles would be small, light and quiet."

"People are living in garages. Lots of folk lost their vehicles.

Many of the roads are impassable. We need to repair the roads. We need to house people immediately."

"We need a vision as we repair things, a small-is-beautiful vision. Big things don't make people any happier."

"You are not seriously considering what is possible and what is impossible."

"After 8000, 9000, 10,000, 12,000, 30,000 earthquakes, anything is possible. An event of this nature requires that we be innovative. We need to answer this, respond to this rugged wilderness Christchurch has become, with our own wildness and creativity."

As they speak, an earthquake cluster happens.

None of them move. The camera guys stay where they are, bounce around a bit, the interviewer keeps talking. An aftershock comes and they keep at it, talking, describing the aftershock. The earthquakes have become an everyday occurrence.

Hemi, "This is an upward thrusting earthquake, a 4.2, 10 metres deep, a shallow earthquake probably centred in the Cashmere Hills area. This is different from the sideways throwing earthquakes which are centred in the Rolleston area."

Hemi looks at his i-pad, "It is Cashmere Hills, epicenter, St Andrews Hill. " There is no wind. It is a still, blue sky, warm sunny earthquake day.

Hemi waves them off. The camera crew and the interviewer disappear deep inside the red zone.

Hemi pinches himself. He looks at the blue blue sky and then he sees his friend the karoro hopping on one leg, looking at him in a quizzical way, all fluffed up. Hemi relaxes and grins back.

Elephants walking, Manchester Street

33

~Maunga~

Mountain
Anchor
hold firm

The nomadic Sea Gypsies of the Burmese archipelago are a wandering water people, who learn to swim before they learn to walk. Norman Dodge describes how they live over half their lives in boats on the open sea where they are often born and die. The children dive down, often thirty feet beneath the water's surface, and pluck clams and sea cucumbers, including small morsels of marine life, and they can see clearly underwater by learning to control the shape of their lens and the size of their pupils, constricting them 22 percent. Most human beings cannot see clearly underwater because as sunlight passes through the water, it is refracted or bent.

Before the tsunami of 26 December 2004 hit the Indian Ocean killing hundreds of thousands, the Sea Gypsies observed that the sea had begun to recede in a strange way and this drawing back was followed by an unusually small wave. They saw dolphins swim quickly to deeper water while elephants stampeded to higher ground. They heard the cicadas fall silent.

The Sea Gypsies began telling each other their ancient story about "The wave that eats people", saying it had come again. Some of the Sea Gypsies fled inland from the shore, moving to higher ground. Those at sea, went out into very deep water. They all survived. The Sea Gypsies put all these unusual events together and saw the whole, using an exceptionally wide-angle lens. Burmese boatmen were also at sea when these pre-natural events were occurring, but they did not survive. A Sea Gypsy was asked how it was that Burmese, who also knew the sea, all perished. He replied, "They were looking at squid. They were not looking at anything. They saw nothing. They looked at nothing. They don't know how to look."

In "Waka Moana", Nainoa Thompson, a Hokule'a Navigator, describes navigation to Sam Low — "Navigation is about understanding and watching nature. Everything you need to guide you is in the ocean, but you need to be skilled enough to see it. It took many years to learn the ocean's many faces, to sense subtle clues, the slight difference in swells, in the colours of the water, in the shape of the clouds and in the movement of the winds."

Pieter is walking to the spot where Kay was found. He plans to sit there to try and get things in perspective. Try to put things back together again. Or maybe nothing will go back together, maybe things will fall in a different way from what he has known. He can't manage to go on like this in the old way. He can't find himself, recall himself, or bring himself to order. It doesn't work at all, none of his old strategies help, and Kay is not here to help him either.

Pieter is walking, slowly and steadily up and into the hills. He gets onto the track between Dyers Pass Rd and Hackthorne Rd. He reaches the Sign of the Takahe, Harry Ell's first castle resting place, and rests in the garden there on a seat beside the walled-off damaged castle. Then he is up and on his way again. There's a storm brewing. Rain comes sideways into his face.

He doesn't care. He has good shoes and good protective gear on and he doesn't care. There isn't anything more the earth or the sky can do to him. The bouncing rolling rocks have taken Kay. Some rocks have weird patterns of cracks down their sides or across their surface, as if some person had been drawing in a foreign script across the rock. As in a house, the patterns can reveal severe structural damage hidden beneath the surface. Sometimes such damage is not detectable at all.

Disaster comes at different moments in people's lives, Pieter thinks. It could have happened when they were young and newly married. It could have happened when he was a young boy, or a teenager, or when he was an old man and Kay an old woman, alive and with him. Or the earthquakes could have come when they were both dead and in their graves, or before they were born.

But the earthquakes are happening now and they have taken Kay, and Pieter is inconsolable. He is doing his best, but some days he struggles to put one foot in front of the other and these last few days he has wanted to do nothing, nothing at all. He wants simply to lie down beside Kay and never get up again.

His body aches, as if he were bound around his ankles and his wrists. Sometimes his fingers ache and his head is foggy. Today a band across his shoulders aches as if he were carrying a cross on his back. He knows these are all to do with Kay's passing and with the constant aftershocks he is dealing with as best he knows how. But he feels his best is no longer good enough. Enough is enough. These earthquakes have gone on far too long, well over a year now, and still going strong.

He doesn't want to be anywhere else. He has no intention of doing that. Kay died here. His mother has died. They are buried here in this broken city. This is where they lived, they laughed together, played, made love, talked, walked, and this is where he is going to stay.

Pieter was pulling down one chimney and it looked all sound and straight up and down, not a tipping anywhere to be seen. But he got below the roofline. Two layers of brick had been ground evenly into dust by the shaking. The entire top of the chimney sat, straight up and down, on ground up dust. Another shake and it would have collapsed right through the house into their living room or bedroom. He wonders if he looks okay on the surface, but underneath he is like that chimney.

Pieter can understand Hemi wanting to go someplace else, but that is not in his book. Hemi is young. The world is his oyster. He can go anywhere, do anything, fall in love maybe.

Pieter stays on the track at first and then he turns off and goes over the fences where they have blocked off access in case of more rock fall. He walks up and across the tussock grasslands, through the manuka and old man pine to the place. He sits down at the spot where they found Kay lying. He stays there.

No enlightenment comes bolting through Pieter, but slowly he feels like his head is clearing and he is rising out of it all. The responsibilities of the last months fall from his shoulders. The aches in his body become fainter. He feels younger. A kahu flies high above him. He watches the kahu for a long time. He watches the kahu soar high up into the sky and then circle down and down and down. Then up again the kahu goes straight up on a shaft of wind.

He would love to be on the back of the kahu flying high in the sky. The storm is blowing all around them. Pieter hardly notices the storm. He is with the kahu flying as if from a great height. He can see all over the mountains, the harbour, the city, and all the way out to the great Pacific. He is flying with the kahu on these wild currents of wind and ocean breeze, the rain barely wetting his tail feathers. She screeches with delight as she winds down on a wind funnel. Then when the sleet comes she finds a big rocky overhang and hides herself under there.

He thinks of all the wonder-filled times he had together with Kay and he is thankful for the time they did have together. When there is a clearing in the weather, he picks himself up from under the rocky outcrop and walks along the ridgeline of the Cashmere Hills. He knows that Kay watches out for him.

Pieter walks swiftly along the track. He knows that it would be better if Hemi stayed, but it is all right if he goes. Hemi must do what is in his heart to do. Pieter walks across the slopes and then turns and heads down the hill to the Sign of the Takahe and home.

Seal on Rock, Scarborough

34

~Rapanui~

Waka sternpost
Flash, split open
Sheet lightning

Prior to the 1931 Napier Hastings earthquake, the local tohunga who was watching the ocean, saw a mako, a white shark swimming right in the Napier waterfront area. He put out an alert to all the iwi and folk he knew in the area and suggested they head to a marae south of Napier Hastings, so they would be safe. No Maori people perished in the Napier Hastings earthquakes in 1931.

In "Time and The Forest," Peter Hooper writes in 1981, about a massive earthquake hitting Christchurch and two young boys from the West Coast coming over and exploring the remains of the great city. Peter Hooper lived in Greymouth. He writes about a huge earthquake destroying Christchurch years thirty years before it happens.

After the earthquakes I met Dr. Vivienne Burrows an older Christchurch lady who was a scientist who had studied with Ernest Rutherford in Christchurch and then in England. She later returned to live in Christchurch. She had been in Cashel Street at Ballantynes the day before the earthquake and parked her car by the river. When she got to the river, all the water was flowing down the centre of the river, and the mud at the sides of the river was plopping like the hot pools in Rotorua. She went home and wrote it all down that night, the night before the first one, the 4 September 2010 earthquake.

A Qi Gong master is sitting meditating in Christchurch through a severe earthquake. His body is waving like a willow waves in the wind.

The earth asks that we become active participants. The earth insists on all of us becoming alert, interacting with the earth quaking, the lights dancing, the birds singing, the earth waking, listening with every inch, every pore of our being.

Hemi goes out to Rapanui and sits on the sand gazing at the big broken rock. "Eh, Rapanui, I thought I knew how to be a man in the world. Hone has died. When I was younger he helped me grow up, into the world. The cliff face yells, tells me off. The cliff face sounds like my brother, wants me to change from being a taurekareka rascal to being a kaitiaki guardian. I understand.

The people hear the sound of her shaking, but they don't understand what she is saying. I tell them we have no choice, not when the cliff face yells like that. They don't get it. We have to move now and change simply and swiftly our way of acting in the world.

Eh, Rapanui you were a fist, an ure, a prow, thrusting upward into the sky, a strong place for me to turn to. Now you are open wide like a chalice. You reveal your softness, your feminine side, as you have never done before. These earthquakes that have turned us inside out and upside down, have transformed you." Hemi turns and walks back up from the place where the waves lap the sand.

The tide is way out. Tess is sitting on the rock wall above the estuary looking at the yacht dipping up and down on the outgoing tide. She sees a shag disappear into the depths and watches to see where it will rise again. It takes ages. She thinks maybe she has missed it, lost it. Then she sees the shag some way off rise up out of the water again, moving fast against the tide. Tess wonders which way she herself is going. She can't bear the thought of moving at all. She has already moved here from Guangzhou and she has no desire to move again anywhere. She likes the people here. They are so friendly and kind. They have fed her and sheltered her and helped her, and she knew none of them before. She feels like she belongs here. And she can't get him out of her mind, the young man with the green brown eyes who can hear her thinking.

She has no job. She has never ever not had a job. Even when she was at school she had a part-time job helping in a nursery. She picks her way along the side of the estuary wall, heading for Rapanui. What else can she do, but listen to the rain falling softly, sink inside the deep dark blue night sky, follow the cycles of the stars, the moon, and the sun. She sees someone moving around near Rapanui.

Tuawera, Cave Rock

35

~Tuawera~

Cave rock
Heat from long
ago

During the 30,000 earthquakes, many of us have a near death experience. We ourselves or friends or family members or workmates, die or are injured or become ill, or we lose our homes, or have seriously damaged homes, or lose our work, our workplaces, or our businesses. The central city is demolished piece by piece. Thousands of homes are red stickered due to liquefaction, rising rivers, or falling rocks. Yet most of us are still here.

Some of us uproot and shift, wishing never to return. Ten thousand people move into the province of Canterbury, which surrounds Christchurch. These small Canterbury villages are experiencing booms with new shops, theatres, cafes, businesses, and manufacturing. Yet most of us stay here in Christchurch living on this erratic, sometimes raging, storm heaving, sometimes calm and peaceful, ocean earth.

The quakes take us into the world at another level. We can't escape their depth, their insight, their excursions into death and dying and life and living. Material things no longer matter. Things break, things are only things.

One person only needs so many things to live a happy life. You don't need anything like the number of things we accumulate. What we need and what we don't need, ruthlessly and quickly decided for us. Those of us who can, make our peace around the possession of things, we make do without things. We let those things that are broken, go. We move on.

We ourselves are not as we appear. Folk might think we look the same as we once did. A little more stressed maybe, busier, more preoccupied fixing things up, tending the injured and those who have become sick in the wake of the quake. Some folk come here to give us a foot up, a helping hand. But it's hard to find a place to start, a way in, how to make an ordinary move here, how to lift a finger, wriggle a toe, without being catapulted up and into the sky.

In "Taking Appearance Seriously", Henri Bortoft says Goethe was concerned with how we experience nature with our senses as it comes into being. He describes creating a space so we can receive the phenomenon instead of trying to grasp it, so we become a participant in the coming-into-being of the phenomenon instead of an onlooker who is separate from it.

Franz Kafka writes, "You do not have to leave your room. Remain sitting at your table and listen. You do not even need to listen, simply wait. Do not even wait, be quiet, still and solitary. The world will freely offer itself to you to be unmasked. It has no choice, it will roll in ecstasy at your feet."

Is this what she is doing, our living breathing earth, our earth mother Papatuanuku, rolling in ecstasy at our feet? And all we need to do is make sure we are in no mortal danger, then be quiet and still, watch and listen.

Tess sits down and waits at the rock by the track, she waits for Hemi to come to her. She wants to rush into his arms and hold him tight, but she waits. He waves.

"Hi Hemi."

"Tess."

"You like this place?"

"I do."

"I will miss you, Hemi."

"I don't know why I am thinking of going. I don't know what has come over me."

"You have a good job, your flat is all right to live in, not wrecked like some people's places."

"I study the fault lines, and that is the difficulty. It is like reading the earth. I listen hard, to try and understand her shaking, her quaking, her rolling over in her sleep."

"And what is she saying?"

"It could go on and on, Tess. This is a very unusual sequence of earthquakes. The Inangahua 7.1 earthquake that rocked the West Coast in 1968 was huge and did great amounts of damage up and down the Coast, but it was followed by aftershocks that progressively settled down, following the big one. The two plates were rubbing together. This earthquake sequence is a breaking, a cracking open of the plate. In this scenario, we have brand new faults opening up, different sequences layered one on top of the other and unusually, all circling around the same place, Christchurch."

"None of the quakes have been greater than the first one."

"They have been bigger than 6 and much more damaging than the first one because of where the fault lines sit and how shallow the quakes are, and the type of earth, rock, sediment and clay."

"So, what are we are meant to do?"

" Clean up the polluted rivers, estuaries, harbours, and ocean beaches. Stop putting shit into our waterways, so fish and ducks can live in there again. Clean the polluted skies. Stop taking coal, oil and gas out of the bowels of the earth and burning them so their gases rise up into the sky. No fracking, no oil exploration, no oil drilling. Monitor cattle farting. Be moderate in the numbers of stock we keep. Regenerate native forests and swamp lands so birds and fish can dwell safely here. Care for farms and gardens without poisoning the earth. Don't build above six stories high. Build safe buildings in wood and steel. None of this is hard. It is a shift in our way of doing."

"You think we just do it?"

"This morning the interviewer said it was impossible. He looked at me as if I had lost the plot. They wouldn't even contemplate one of these changes. They say we have to fix everything, back to the way it was. This is everything. This is where we start from the bottom up. "

"Trust yourself, Hemi. Keep true to yourself. Trust what you see. Hemi."

"I shall go back and have another conversation with them.

Are you all right, Tess?"

"I am recovering, Hemi."

Tess smiles and lets Hemi take her hand in his. Tess and Hemi wander on up the beach toward Tuawera, the great whale, Cave Rock.

Crack, Estuary

36

~Tangaroa~

Atua of the Ocean

Planet Neptune

Some folk think it is not the sea that moves in a high tide, but the land beneath the sea that moves to create a high tide. So when the high tide is up, the land sinks down and when it is low tide, the land rises. After experiencing the earthquake period, this feels possible. It is the land beneath the ocean and beneath our feet that is rising and falling. The water simply follows the movement of the land.

When the moon is full and in perigee, is the time when you take care not to be out on the ocean in wild seas. Full moon or new moon perigee is the time when you tie everything and everyone down for safety.

The moon is the closest celestial body to us here on earth. In Bali, every full moon and every new moon people gather at the temples and pray and sing and eat together. They are conscious of and attend as a people to the movement of the moon.

Like the sun, the moon affects our atmosphere, our tides and our bodies. With the quakes I watch the movement of the moon more closely.

This is Ruaumoko, the unborn child of Papatuanuku, awakening, twisting and turning inside the belly of Papatuanuku. These earthquakes, volcanoes, tsunamis, are the earth talking, communicating to us, describing to us the way forward.

When folk are pulled up and out of the rubble, covered in dust and mortar, standing up, walking, almost whole, buried alive for hours and hours, they have this look in their eyes of otherworldliness, as if they have come back from the dead. Folk walk around more relaxed now, but some still have this look in their eyes. Other people have this look too.

In January 2012, a year and five months after the very first big one, my cousin was under a bus, had jacks and all the works holding up the bus. He was trying to fix something he forgets what now, no, he doesn't want to remember. For some odd reason he thought it was important enough to lie under a bus. Anyways there he was lying on the ground on his back under a bus all the way under.

And suddenly the earth went wavy, big waves rippling through the earth. On his back he began pulling himself out from under the bus as fast as he could. The bus teetered there back and forth on those blocks teetering and teetering. He moved faster than he'd ever moved in his life, like lightning. He pulled his last foot out and then the bus crashed to the ground. Nobody else was in the factory. He was there late, on his own, trying to fix the bus up for the next day. He doesn't know who saved his life that day, but someone got him out of there alive. He has the look in his eyes.

I wonder if most of us all have this look in our eyes, in varying intensities. Like butterflies newly born out of the cocoon. It is a look of terror, of awe, of wonder. Do all of us have this look?

Pieter is walking home from the city along the edge of Hagley Park. The daffodils are out in their yellow and white splendour. The wind is blowing through them turning their heads. He walks with a spring in his step. Spring is good for his heart and his soul, his mind and his blood. He whistles to himself as he passes the netball courts and turns down towards St Mary's Church Square.

Maybe, he thinks, he could start afresh, start something new. He feels like the spring is in his blood, in his bones. He walks across St Mary's Square under the trees. Hemi is sitting dumbfounded, under a tree, his long legs sticking out. Pieter is not looking where he is going. He stumbles over Hemi's feet.

"You all right there, Hemi?"

Hemi looks up at Pieter as if coming out of a reverie, shakes his head, blinks his eyes,

"All right, all right."

Pieter sits down near Hemi.

"What's up Hemi?"

"Nothing, nothing," Hemi says absentmindedly as if he is not here at all but someplace else a million miles away. Hemi picks a dandelion and starts picking the yellow petals off. He squeezes a bit of juice out of the stem.

"There's a lot of things going on, Hemi."

"I'm worn out."

"Things will settle down sooner or later. Anything else up?"

"I went roaring in with the camera crew this morning like I'd seen a vision."

"People do see visions from time to time."

"Sure, Pieter."

"What did you say this morning?"

"I said we have to change things radically here, run the whole city on clean green electrical energy. That there's a surplus of electricity in the South Island and there's no need for us to import any dirty fuels at all. We can do all this straight away. There's nothing stopping us. Clean up our waterways, bring all the fish back. Clean up the air."

"What is wrong with any of that?"

"They think it's impossible. We've got enough on our hands. I just kept on and on."

"Are you still planning to leave?"

"I didn't tell them I was going to leave."

"Are you going to?"

"They will sack me anyhow."

"Hmm. I wonder how on earth we could start to implement your ideas?"

"Maybe I could unpack them one idea at a time. You think what we have already done. In ordinary times it would have taken 5 to 10 years to regroup the broken secondary schools moving them in with the unbroken ones. It took 3 weeks. The time is ripe for cleaning up the water, the air, planting forest gardens, regenerating old forests. Not such a mission as it would have been."

"We need to stretch our thinking a little, open our minds wider."

"I think these big earthquakes encourage us to change quickly and radically, to think fluently, with our eyes wide open, with receptive bodies and minds. It's not a bad thing. You been talking with Mary again, Pieter?"

"Of course."

Hemi laughs. "She is a source of great inspiration to you, Pieter."

"Our Lady is to do with hope and a way forward in the face of all aridity and disenchantment."

"Maybe I should try having a yak with her, but I doubt if she'd bother with a disbeliever like me."

"She doesn't mind who shows up, Hemi."

Hemi sits up.

"You know Pieter there's a big container sitting along the road on an empty section and there's nothing much in it and it's not doing anything."

"That big yellow one?"

"Yes. I was looking at it and thinking a few days back, that we could sorely do with your shop up and running again. I miss it and so does the whole neighbourhood. We all miss your shop."

"I miss the people coming and going with their big woes and their small joys."

"Do you think you could set up your shop again in the yellow container?"

"I could rent it from you?"

"It's yours, Pieter, you can have it."

"I'll pay you rent."

"Forget the rent."

"But, Hemi!"

"We need our shop again."

“I’ll do it. I will re-open the shop in the yellow container. Put up a big sign. Let everyone know I am re-opening!”

Hemi and Pieter stand and shake hands on the deal and head homewards making plans as they go regarding the positioning of the yellow container that is to become Pieter’s new shop.

Punga, Tuam Street

37

~Tāwhiri-mātea~

Atua of Clouds
Wind, Hail
Snow, Storms

Bob Gordon studied and worked with the Australian Victorian bushfire survivors. He says the danger passes, but deep inside our tissues, the cortisol keeps running in our systems. We can't stop, we become hyper, or we freeze, we can't go on. We are like divers inside a decompression chamber coming out of the bends. And we've got them bad.

This stress doesn't stop even though the danger has passed. We have disturbed sleep, poor sleep patterns, and memory loss. We can't feel anything for anyone, even for ourselves. We get a range of small physical and mental ailments. We can't think straight. We worry about random things. We can have an identity crisis. Who am I, what am I here for, why am I with you, who are you, who am I?

I wonder where I lie on Bob Gordon's spectrum. The cure? He suggests rest, relax each day, pray, walk, meditate, sing, dance, eat together, pick flowers, lie on the beach in the sun, swim, lie under a tree by a river, read a book, tell stories, recite ballads around the fire, play tennis, garden, do outside things, don't hang around screens too much. Take at least two or three days off every week. Change your pace, slow down.

I wonder how on earth we do this in the face of all the things that need to be done, the repairs, the throwing out of broken things, and the relocations.

I am lost, lost in time, lost in space. I have no idea how to proceed in this new world. I go to the re-opened library, find an excellent book. I get a rug and settle myself down under a tree with a cup of tea, and read the book. I know that recovery from these major happenings does not happen overnight.

I know that half of the underground workings of the city are damaged. I know that my insides could be in just the same way. I can hear the earthquakes in the voices of people when we speak to each other. I can hear the tremor, the quaking of the earth inside people's voices, see the quaking inside people's movements.

I decide to do nothing at all. I hope when I have finished doing nothing, it will become apparent to me what I have to do next. I sit by the muddy filthy river with the polluted water signs up on its bank, Don't walk in, Don't swim, Don't drink this water. It is polluted. Polluted from broken underground pipes everywhere. The polluted river is depressing with not a fish, nor a duck in sight. If you were a fish or a duck you wouldn't want to be here.

A quake comes and I watch the tree branches sway and the folk walking, gathering and commenting on the intensity of the quake 4.2, 4.6, no, a Magnitude 4.4. People have become accurate at describing the intensity of the quakes as they occur. As long as it's not bubbling-up-earth or a cliff face falling down on you, or a river rising and changing course and running down your street, if you are outside not inside buildings, the earthquake doesn't feel so intense.

Maybe the earthquake makes a hole in the ground, and you move out of the way of the hole and later fill it in with a bit of earth. Even the shaking feels different when you are standing, sitting or lying outside on the earth and you are moving with the earth, not fighting to stand up or trying to get away from something falling.

Tess came in on the wind. She arrived from Asia in a plane on the night of the very first earthquake 3 September 2010, at 10.00pm at night, in the dark. She had never set foot in New Zealand before. She shifted in, and had a job organised to work in a bank. She has never seen the Christchurch streets the way they once were, the city orderly and erect, the chimneys upright, the brick and stone buildings all as they were.

She arrived on that first night, the night when everyone wakes up and runs out onto the streets in their night attire. Candles, tiny windup radios, torches, in hands, waiting outside by torchlight far away from the houses, so when the next one comes folk are well away from the falling masonry and brick chimneys.

Folk trying to locate the epicenter, is it Wellington? Is it the West Coast? Is it Te Anau?

On her first night in the city, in the country, she finds herself walking from house to house, checking there are no injured people inside. The next day she is taking bricks off each roof, picking bricks out of the gardens, out of the lawns, off the streets, taking out broken windows, picking up and throwing out broken crockery. Some of the chimneys, some of the fences, some of the brick walls look perfectly intact from the outside, straight up and down. But she gets herself inside the roof and looks down a wall and a whole layer of brick or stone has been reduced to a thick layer of dust.

She helps work on chimneys and walls for a week, until her job begins. She works and eats with the other helpers. She helps dismantle one chimney after the other. She becomes an expert chimney dismantler.

One day she goes out to the streets covered in mud and slush where the soil has broken up and bubbled up like the hot pools — all around those houses along Avonside Drive, by the Avon River. She isn't surprised at all, she just joins in as if this is the most ordinary sort of thing you do when you shift to another city. It is as if she has been called here on a secret errand, known only to herself. It is as if she was born to be here in this place at this time, and she stays.

After she is buried in the rubble in the city centre at her place of work, she finds it hard to get things back together again. Her job disappears along with the building where she worked. She takes a while to recover from her injuries, but she doesn't want to leave. She wants to stay. It is as if the earthquakes, the people of the city and the city itself have all become an intrinsic part of her. She has no desire to return home, nor to be anywhere else. She feels that she belongs.

She reminds Pieter of how his mother Helena was in her younger days. She just gets on with things, as if she was born to be here now in this place at this time, as if her whole life, this crisis is what she was waiting for. She has a good energy about her, and a clear mindedness. She offers to work as a shop assistant in Pieter's new shop to help get it up and running. Pieter is delighted.

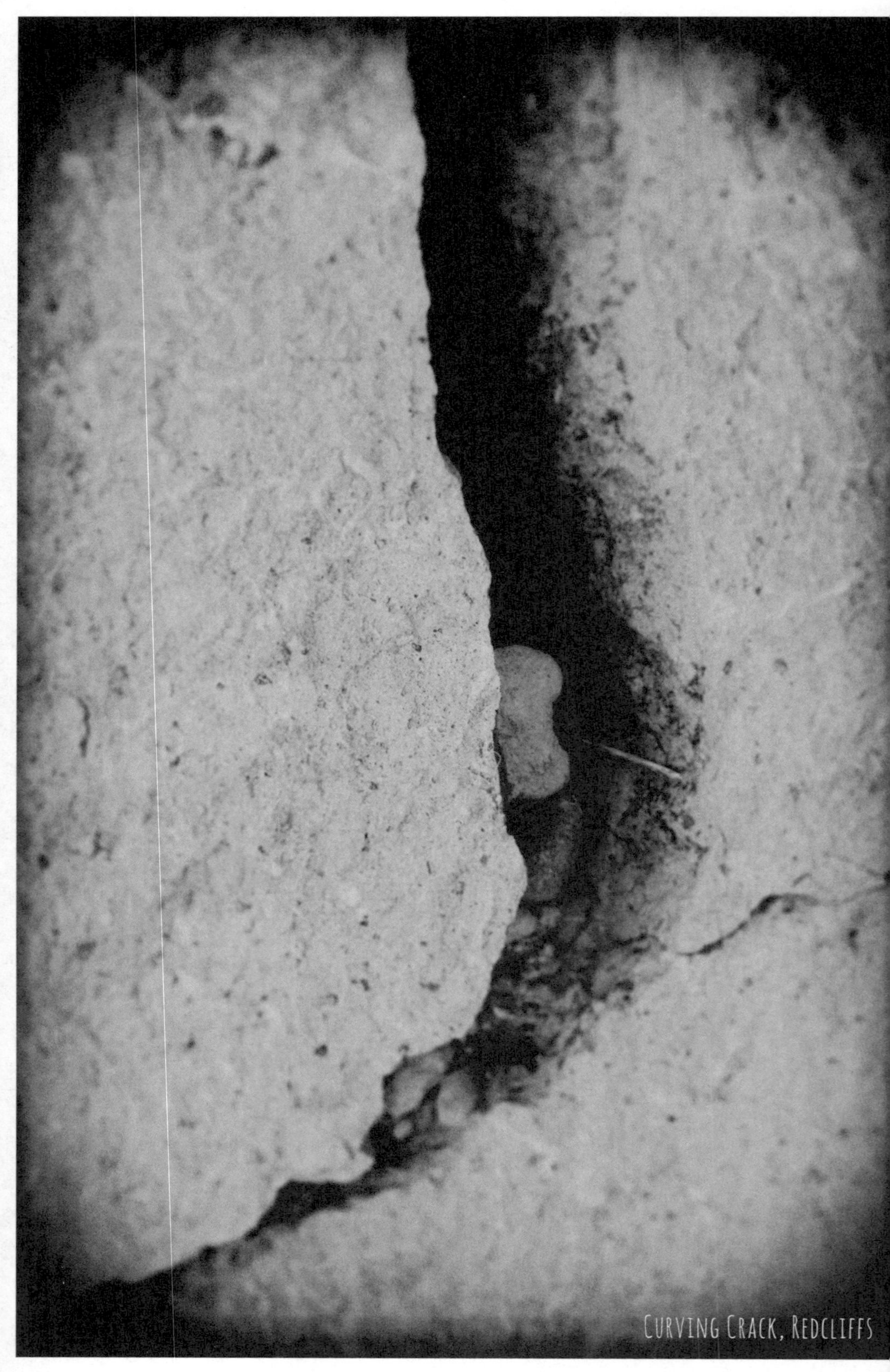

Curving Crack, Redcliffs

38

~Whanaua~

be born
be produced
be brought forth

The streets are paved with mud and debris. Scrawling roughly tarred lines, openings, cracks, sometimes wide enough to see through, to drop through, snake through the streets like ancient hieroglyphics. As if Papatuanuku, our Earth, is trying to speak intimately to us in a language we may understand. After all we make these scrawling marks on paper in the hope someone will read them and make sense of them. She makes the marks in the hope that one or other of us will be able to make sense of her movement. Slim vein-like lines to-ing and fro-ing, in and out, and all around about, in the hope that someone somewhere will make sense of, understand, and see the big picture. The korimako in the walnut tree whistles on, insistent that we hear his birdsong.

I gaze towards the polluted river and see a duck standing on the edge and a tiny swallow-like bird with royal blue wings and an orange head fly over the duck's head, followed by its mate. The duck watches mesmerised. I watch mesmerised. What on earth does this tiny swallow think of it all?

The tiny royal blue swallow sees a cloud of insects rise above the water. Then more tiny blue and orange swallows join the first one. It has become bird heaven. There are lots more insects around, fewer people. Maybe the birds like it better.

Hemi and Kara catch up at the intersection of Colombo and Hereford. There is a great hole in the ground where a multistoried building once stood. The hole is huge and deep and filling up with water. Any underground foundations here will be deeper and more full of steel than the above ground part of the building. They peer into the great hole and then they move on to what was Cathedral Square.

"When are you off, Hemi?"

"I was planning on a couple of weeks, Whaea."

"I hope your plans are going well."

"I've changed my plans."

"Are you going to a different place now?"

"More than that."

"Are you shifting some place else for good, not just for a short time?"

"No, Whaea. I plan to stay here."

"Truly?"

"I am staying right here."

"That's fine by me, Hemi. It's great news." Kara looks at Hemi sideways. She gives him a hug.

"It's good you are staying, Hemi. Those ideas you had the other day, the way forward. I think they are very good ideas. Maybe we could look at how to implement those ideas of yours, Hemi."

Hemi stops in his tracks.

"Why the sudden change, Whaea? You were opposed to even the thought of them."

"I was wrong Hemi. I was thinking only of myself. You are right, we have to think of the young ones coming on. We are only here for a short time. No point trying to make ourselves extinct."

Hemi takes Kara's hand in his. They hongi, nose to nose, breath joining with breath.

Bike market & free repairs High St

39

~Mūwharu~

Caterpillar

I dream I am a caterpillar crawling from leaf to leaf, twig to twig. That is all I have ever known. Then one day the twig on which I placed myself and stayed for a very long time, snaps, breaks in two.

Within seconds of the twig cracking, I find myself naked, bare of my cocoon, I find myself flying through the air. I find that instead of legs I am developing wings.

Instead of a striped furry body, I am developing velvet wings that dance and weave colours in the light. My body can float in air. I am learning to fly, to float in air, to drift in sky. Occasionally I nibble a leaf, but I am not desperate anymore for the leaves the way I was when I was a caterpillar.

The bright yellow container hovers in the air over the spot where it is to be placed in Pieter's front yard. Hemi is directing the driver of the crane and Pieter is waiting for it to land, well back. Hemi puts thumbs up. The large bright yellow container settles down comfortably in his front yard. The crane backs off. Pieter and Hemi head for the front doors of the container. Pieter has shelving ready to go in. Hemi and Tess are there at the ready. Together they help Pieter install the shelving and the counter, and clean everything thoroughly until it looks spotless and new. Pieter is beaming ear to ear.

Kara arrives with a basket of fresh sandwiches filled with avocado, tomato, lettuce, hardboiled eggs, chutney and parsley, for lunch. Tess has brought a great bowl of oranges, apples, bananas and kiwifruit. After lunch they stack the shelves with the stock Pieter has, all ready to go. It even feels a bit like his old broken shop, the way it once was.

Pieter is happy, he sings, "*Als de lente komt dan stuur ik jou tulpen uit Amsterdam* When spring comes I will send you tulips from Amsterdam

Als de lente kmot pluk ik voor jou tulpen uit Amsterdam When spring comes I will pick for you tulips from Amsterdam

Als ik wederkom dan bren ik jou tulpen uit Amsterdam when I return I will bring you tulips from Amsterdam

Duizend gele, duizend rooie wensen jou het allermooiste A thousand yellow ones, a thousand red ones, wish you the very best

Wat m'n mond niet zeggen kan zeggen tulpen uit Amsterdam What my mouth cannot say tulips from Amsterdam will say."

When all of the shelves are up and all of the stock and food is stacked neatly on the shelves and the task is complete, Pieter asks that they gather together to say a special prayer of thanks to Our Lady.

Then Kara offers a karakia asking for blessings for the families of all those who have died. She asks for help from those who have died, for this part of the journey through the brokeness that is Otautahi Christchurch and into the creation of something new.

Together they thank God, Mary and all the Atua, for helping make this new thing possible, this small new bright yellow shop, in the midst of the destruction.

Monarch Butterfly

40

~Wairua atua~

Butterfly

Everything has changed. I rise on the air higher and higher into the sky. My relationship to air, to breeze, to wind current, to heat, to cold air, all of these things have changed irrevocably. Some days I can't remember how it was when I was a caterpillar. I see other caterpillars walking around on the ground or on a branch or a leaf or a twig. And I wonder just how it is for them.

Unable to move freely through the air, they move along on the ground, or on the branch of tree or a leaf, but they don't float or fly into the air. Often they are so obsessed with their own dimension that they have no way of understanding or even contemplating how it is for us, for butterflies, for birds, for wasps, bumble bees and flies.

Time changes too, when I take to the air, it moves swiftly and jumps sometimes backwards, sometimes forwards, sometimes moving spatially. It is hard to explain it to the caterpillars, it is hard to get inside their head to explain what you could see, if you weren't a caterpillar. It is impossible to describe to them what could happen to them too, if the branch they were living on, cracked.

Most caterpillars think they will just die and they don't know much about death. Many of them think if you die you are just dead and that is that. Very few of them ever notice a butterfly or how butterflies drift and fly in the air, they are so busy with their own lives, in their own dimension.

I am a butterfly. I am no longer a caterpillar. Flying is something I never truly pondered when I was a caterpillar. It's strange now looking at caterpillars, knowing they don't watch air currents, small flurries of wind, the circling of the eddying, the flowing, the down winds, the up winds, the winds that come and blow you sideways. I learn to ride on the back of wind. Caterpillars don't seem aware that even on a seemingly windless day, the air is moving.

When I first become a butterfly I learn to fly, like a baby learning to use her body, one bit at a time, arms, hands, feet, legs. I don't fly straight away. Moving in the air is quite different from moving along the earth. The air gets inside me. I move, I flow with her, let her eddy and flow around me. I can't beat and beat my wings and expect to rise up on the air and fly. I need to understand air.

Air moves through and around and with me. My wings move with air. I become light, feathery and floating. My wings are so delicate they can fly apart if I don't move wholly with air. I see things from many different angles. To caterpillars it seems that butterflies appear and disappear at whim. Death for caterpillars is not the end. It is a shifting into a different realm.

I fly up into the ti kouka. I hide there in the heart of its strong flaxen leaves, well away from two enormous blue kereru with proud white breasts, who have been practicing their Holy Spirit dives from the old black matai tree in the valley. They go up, up, up and then turn and fly, facing headfirst to the earth. Just at the end they spin up and out of the dive and land in the ti kouka. They can't resist diving, those beautiful big blue kereru, the biggest and most beautiful doves in the world.

The shape of my wing is the shape of a human's ear. I can listen with my wings. The shape of the magnitude and intensity of the earthquakes is my shape, imprinted on the ground. The geonet map of the 22 February 2011 earthquake's intensity, has the shape and colours of a beautiful butterfly spreading her yellow, orange, red wings across the city of Otautahi Christchurch.

Thank You

Thank you to my precious family, dear friends, neighbours and loving people of Christchurch, who have broken down, wept, walked, prayed, rallied, sang, fled, picked flowers, talked, suffered, shared stories, meals and cups of tea, living through these earth shattering events together with me. Your pain, warmth, resilience, creativity, courage and love have inspired this story.

Special thanks to Maurice Gray for the karakia on page 14, Aroha Yates-Smith for her waiata "Kake ake" on page 71 and "Whakarongo" on page 150, Owen Dippie for painting the two murals of the ballerina depicted on page 158 and the elephants on page 182, and Rone for painting the face on the wall mural on page 164. Thank you to Elizabeth O'Connor, Ross Gumbley and Philip Aldridge at the Court Theatre, Creative New Zealand, and the actors Helen Moran, Adam Brookfield, Hannah Gin, Michael Kier Morrissey, Sarah Franks, Lucy Porter, Tainui Kuru, Lauren Marshall, Juliet Reynolds Midgley, Phil Vaughan, Tim Bartlett, Alice Canton, Maree McGuigan, and Nathaniel Ta'ase who workshopped the play "Awakening Ruaumoko", which is intrinsic to this novel.

Thank you Aroha Yates-Smith, Penelope Snowdon, Carolyn Gallagher, Sr Pauline O'Reagan, Fr Patrick Austin Laverty, Moyra Pearce, Jen Rippingale, Bruce Anderson, Liam Gallagher-Power, Barbara Petrie, Patricia Veronese, Amy Paulussen, Margaret Ingram-Melamed, John Weir, Joy Ryan-Bloore, Komene Kururangi and Maree Coffey for your comments and invaluable insights at various stages through the writing process.

Especial thanks to James George for the clarity of the edit, to Michael Coughlan for the eloquence of the photographs, and to Katy Yiakmis for the beauty of the book design and layout.

It has been a privilege to work together with you on this mahi.

Nga mihi aroha Kathleen Gallagher